On the Great Plains

A haunted cabin in the middle of the wild great plains? Not exactly, but that was the way the pretty little slip of a girl, Kate McCallister, characterized it when young Ben Flowers appeared to take possession of the property. When she showed him the hundred or so bullet holes in the cabin walls, he understood what she meant. The place was shadowed by many violent memories, and some of them were to return to haunt it again.

It was Ben's first and maybe only chance to build a life of his own and, if it was necessary, he was determined to fight off the spectres of the past with the cold steel of his own guns.

By the same author

The Devil's Canyon
The Drifter's Revenge
West of Tombstone
On The Wapiti Range
Rolling Thunder
The Bounty Killers
Six Days to Sundown
Rogue Law
The Land Grabbers

On the Great Plains

Logan Winters

ROBERT HALE · LONDON

First published in Great Britain 2009

ISBN 978-0-7090-8736-6

Robert Hale Limited
Clerkenwell House
Clerkenwell Green
London EC1R 0HT

www.halebooks.com

Typeset by
Derek Doyle & Associates, Shaw Heath
Printed and bound in Great Britain by
CPI Antony Rowe, Chippenham and Eastbourne

ONE

The starlight striking the snowfield lit it with a strange blue glow as it glimmered away into the distances. The wind was strong at the backs of the three riders as they approached the low-built cabin made of unbarked logs, plastered in its chinks with Dakota mud. It was a stretch even to call the poor shack a cabin.

The three men slowed their weary mounts as they neared the cabin. If there had been any way to avoid the shack, any human contact, they would have preferred it, but they were half frozen and their horses needed rest and food. A stubble field poking through the snow gave evidence that there had been oats or perhaps alfalfa growing here once. Now scythed against the coming winter, presumably baled and stored it might offer their ponies, angry now and fitful as they plowed through the hock-deep snow, a chance to be properly fed.

The cabin had no windows, only two gun slits cut into the front wall to provide firing holes against Indian attacks. A tendril of smoke curled up to meet the night sky from the rough stone chimney, and in the gun slits faint lantern light showed, so someone was home.

The three riders approached the house, calling out to it, then swinging down, standing for a minute in the chill of night, their horses' reins in their gloved hands, waiting for a response from within.

'What do you want!' a voice from the sagging cabin replied eventually. The door had not been opened.

'A little warmth, brother!' Calvin Mercer called back. 'And feed for our horses if you've got it. It's been a long ride and a cold one.'

The wait seemed interminable. Young Billy Carter who still wore his yellow-striped cavalry trousers shivered, stamped his feet and watched the door hopefully. Calvin seemed unconcerned. The big man, looking twice his size in the bulky buffalo coat he wore, snarled. 'I'll give 'em another minute, then I'll open the door myself.'

'Steady, Cal,' the third man said. Mercer's rashness was one of the reasons why they found themselves in their present situation. 'They'll open up. How could they turn men away on a night like this?' Billy Carter looked hopefully at the man speaking, trusting his word. Rincon was a heroic figure to young Billy. Nothing seemed to rattle the lanky, mustached man. If there was ever a man to ride the long plains with, it was Rincon.

Calvin Mercer, growing irritable at the long wait, had just placed a boot upon the sagging porch when the door opened a crack and they were eyeballed from within. 'All right,' they were told, 'might as well come in, boys.'

The three tramped across the swaying porch and into the low-ceilinged, smoky cabin. The heat of the hotly burning fire was nearly overwhelming after the bitter cold of the open Dakota plains, and they shucked their long coats quickly.

Billy Carter slipped into a corner near the stone fireplace and turned his back to the crackling flames, studying the men inside the cabin. He felt certain that they had already seen the cavalry trousers he was wearing, imagined that they knew his secrets.

The two men living in the house were similar in appearance – they might have been brothers – both had black beards streaked with gray, deep-set dark eyes and powerful arms. Their expressions were dour. Obviously they had had a long debate about the wisdom of opening the door at all. Obviously neither was satisfied with the decision they had come to. The nearer man held a cup of chicory coffee which he sipped as he approached the new arrivals across the uneven plank floor of the cabin. He halted in front of Calvin Mercer, lowered his cup, squinted at the big man and said, 'Hey! You're—' and his right hand dropped to his holstered pistol.

Calvin shifted his feet, brought up his Colt revolver and shot the man in the throat, sending him stumbling back, falling near the fire. His tin cup clattered free.

'That was sudden,' Rincon said. He had drawn his own revolver to cover the other brother.

'It's a sudden country,' Calvin Mercer said in a growl. He walked to the man he had shot, assured himself that he was dead, frisked his body and turned back to the second man.

'Got hay ricked up out there?' Mercer asked. There was no tremor in his voice. He asked the question as if nothing had happened. Billy Carter, the dead man lying within inches of his boots, found himself trembling, and it was not from the cold. He looked to Rincon for guidance, but Rincon's eyes were unreadable.

'There's some, Mercer,' the bearded landholder answered. There was no dread, no uneasiness in his voice either. Billy felt a boy among men. How far had they ridden from civilization?

'You know who I am then?' Calvin Mercer asked.

'Yes. I knew, too. But I knew better than to draw a gun on you.' The man clicked his tongue, took three strides to stand over the fallen man and shook his head. 'He was my brother, Mercer. I just want you to know there are six of us altogether. You have started something here.'

Calvin looked at the fire, again at the dead

man, holstered his pistol and asked, 'You got anything to eat? I haven't had a meal since Fargo.'

After devouring some kind of pasty stew which seemed to be mostly old potatoes, onions and buffalo meat seasoned with about half a pound of black pepper, Calvin Mercer went out to see to the horses. Billy had been dispatched on his own secret mission: they had to find a safe place to stash the gold, if, as they had been told, there was a chance of four more armed men riding in.

Rincon sat in a chair, its back tilted against the wall, near the glowing fireplace. His blue Colt revolver rested on his lap. He asked the black-bearded man a few careful questions.

'What name do you go by?'

'Deuce. Deuce Whittaker,' the man answered, without glancing at Rincon as he scrubbed the dirty bowls at a bucket in the kitchen.

'Sony about your brother,' Rincon said. 'Cal Mercer is kind of trigger-happy.'

The bearded man, Deuce Whittaker, slammed a tin plate down. Still without turning, he said, 'Yeah. I'm sure it really bothered you. Your name is Rincon, isn't it?'

Rincon did not answer, but he frowned, his

drooping dark mustache rising unevenly. *This* was not good. If the dead brother had recognized Calvin Mercer, it could have been through any of dozens of chance encounters. Now Rincon, too, had been identified. If the men following them were to be pointed in the direction they were going to take, it would be very bad indeed. Perhaps Cal Mercer's apparently abrupt killing of the other brother was more prudent than it had first seemed.

'You said there's six brothers in all,' Rincon commented. He asked languidly, 'Any idea when the others might be coming here?'

'They roam,' Deuce Whittaker said. 'It could be tomorrow, next week, could be in the next hour.'

Rincon nodded. It seemed they had made a big mistake in halting here, but what else could they have done? The night was frigid, the horses exhausted. The door opened to admit Calvin Mercer, carrying their long guns with him. He stacked the rifles in the corner and stood slapping his arms for warmth. He glanced around and asked, 'Where's the kid?'

'Doing what you told him to do,' Rincon answered.

'How about my brother!' Deuce Whittaker demanded. 'Aren't you going to let me bury him?'

'There'll be time when we're gone,' Mercer muttered, moving nearer to the fire.

'He says he doesn't know when his other brothers might he riding in,' Rincon informed Mercer.

'He doesn't, doesn't he?' Calvin Mercer said, flashing Deuce an ugly glance. 'He better hope it's not before we're ready to leave. Those other boys might find that they have two brothers they have to bury.'

Deuce understood the threat for what it was. He returned to the room and sat stolidly in the corner, keeping his bulky arms folded. He wasn't going to try for a gun.

The front door burst open and Billy Carter, wide-eyed,entered. 'I think they've caught up with us!' he said wildly.

'Them? Or the Whittaker brothers!' Cal Mercer asked.

'Can't tell,' Billy answered. He was shaking from head to foot, and not from the cold of the night which drifted into the cabin through the open door. 'There's three, maybe four riders. I caught their silhouettes against the stars while I was doing.' – he glanced at Deuce Whittaker, and grew cautious – 'what you told me to do.'

'All right, boys,' Rincon said rising lazily to his feet, 'let's fort up. The time has come to pay for our sins.'

Peering through a gun slit in the unbarked logs, Rincon saw that it was worse than they had thought. He looked at the eager-eyed Deuce Whittaker and told him, 'It isn't your brothers.'

'The army patrol!' Calvin Mercer said, shouldering Rincon aside so that he could look out the gun slit into the starry night. 'Damn! I was sure we'd lost them.'

'They must have a pretty good Indian scout with them,' Rincon muttered. 'I thought the new snow had covered our tracks well enough.'

'What do we do now?' Billy Carter asked. His nerves were jangling loud enough to he heard.

'Do?' Rincon replied. 'Why we fight them, Bill. It's that or we'll surely hang.'

'We could give up,' Billy said. His face was waxen in the firelight.

'We could. Then your worries would be over . . . except for that firing squad that's waiting for you.'

'Maybe if we gave them back the gold—'

'Then they'd only shoot you for desertion,' Calvin Mercer said derisively. 'You knew what you were getting into when you opened that safe for us. Now, Billy, it's time to pay the piper. If we can fight clear of this place, we've still got a chance. There can't be more than half a dozen of them,' he guessed, still peering out through the gun slit.

'Hand me my Winchester,' Rincon said coldly. 'There's only one way out of this mess.'

Before Mercer had even given him his rifle, the soldiers opened up on the house. They were taking no chances with the fugitives. Bullets peppered the front door, sending splinters flying. The walls were peppered with .45-70 loads from their Springfield rifles. Billy Carter hit the floor.

'Damnit all!' Deuce Whittaker shouted. 'Tell them to hold their fire; you've got a prisoner in here. I have nothing to do with this!'

'You do now,' Calvin Mercer growled. 'Life can be tough, can't it?'

Rincon had shouldered his Winchester and now he levered four shots in a row with it. driving the soldiers to ground.

'Get any?' Mercer asked.

'Might've nicked one. It's too dark for sure shooting.'

It wasn't too dark for the soldiers who had plenty of ammunition and all the time in the world. Also they had a large, unmoving target and they continued to spray the cabin with gunfire. Rincon, and Mercer, who was now positioned at the gun slit on the other side of the door, shot back, aiming for the muzzle flashes from the army patrol's guns.

Not many of the rifles beyond the walls of the tumbledown cabin did any real harm, but the plank door which seemed to be their prime target was taking on the appearance of a sieve as the fight continued. The old rotting wood could not take much more. Nearly a hundred rounds had been aimed at the cabin, and some of these did penetrate, singing off the fireplace stones, cutting deep furrows along the badly plastered walls. One round found its way into the kitchen and drilled a neat hole through Deuce Whittaker's newly scrubbed stew pot. The cabin filled with acrid gunsmoke from the answering weapons that Cal Mercer and Rincon fired until the barrels of their rifles were hot.

'I'm giving up!' a frantic Billy Carter shouted wildly. 'I can't take any more of this. I don't care what they do to me!'

He lunged toward the door, swinging it half open. Cal Mercer caught his arm before he could wriggle through.

'Don't be a fool!' Cal shouted. 'Get down.'

It was too late for that. The snipers beyond opened fire again, and Rincon saw at least two bullets tag flesh. Billy Carter slapped at his forehead as if he had been stung by a bee, but a .45-70 slug had penetrated his skull. Another shot hit Calvin Mercer high on the arm and he spun around, dropping his rifle. Arterial blood spurted from a badly damaged blood vessel and he fell face forward to the plank floor, twitching and kicking.

At Billy's first movement, Deuce Whittaker had leaped to his feet rushing to snatch up his own rifle which he now held on Rincon.

'All right?' he panted at Rincon. 'Now what are you going to do?' They could hear pounding boots approaching. Rincon opened his hand and let his Winchester clatter to the floor.

'Surrender, I guess,' he said, and he took a

seat in the corner chair to wait for the soldiers' arrival.

The first man through the door, an over-eager recruit, startled Whittaker and he turned that way. Deuce had his rifle in his hands, and the young trooper, mistaking the move, shot him dead. His eyes turned toward the mustached man seated in the corner, his hands raised.

'I give it up,' Rincon said quietly.

Then a trio of other soldiers entered, looked at the carnage. They tried to do something for Mercer who was still somehow, alive. They disarmed Rincon who complied with every order placidly.

Eventually a lieutenant, who appeared even younger than the soldier who had shot Deuce Whittaker, entered the room and told Rincon, 'There's going to be hell to pay for this night.'

'I expect so,' Rincon agreed. 'The devil always wants his dues, doesn't he?'

TWO

Benjamin Flowers stepped out of the county recorder's office into the bright spring day, wearing the smile of success. He folded the deed he held in his hand and tucked it into the inside pocket of his worn leather iacket. Then he stood for a minute, taking in the warmth of morning. He allowed himself the time to bask in the pleasure of his achievement even knowing that there were months, years of toil and trouble ahead.

He meant to have breakfast and then shake the dust of Fargo from his heels. He wanted to be riding . . . *home* to his newly purchased ranch north of Pawnee. Ben Flowers was only twenty-six years of age, but he had been on his own since he was fourteen and he had worked every one of those years, saving his money while the men around him squandered theirs on whiskey and at the gambling tables. They had mocked him at times, but he was steadfast in his determination: one day he would have a place of his own.

And now he did.

Half a section of Dakota land with a structure already on it. He couldn't resist glancing at the deed in his pocket once more. It was true. The land had been put up at auction after the former owner had been delinquent in paying taxes for the five previous years. A notice in the *Fargo Times* had caught Ben's eye. The auction had been scantly attended and his bid of $513 dollars had been accepted. So Ben Flowers, former cowhand and roughneck, now was the owner of 320 acres of Dakota land. He hadn't seen the property. He was working on instinct, but instinct told him that if the former owner had taken the time to erect a building of some sort – undefined in the notice – it must have shown some promise as a ranch.

No matter, he would continue to be optimistic until proven wrong. He was young and had the time and strength to invest to try to prove up on the land. In time . . . well, a lot of things might happen in time, but he would not let concern darken his thoughts on this bright, sunny morning. All of the hard labor lay ahead; for today he would not let anything darken his mood. He was walking on clouds as he crossed the dusty street, dodging a freight wagon and a pair of racing cowboys on their cutting horses.

Entering the shaded stable to reclaim his sorrel pony, he felt that nothing could be as fine as the way he felt on this morning. Then it became even brighter, warmer.

He had slipped the pony its bit and smoothed the saddle blanket when he lifted his head at approaching footsteps to see the pretty blonde girl in the blue gingham dress walking toward him, her expectant eyes on him. Slender, she was, but attractively built. Her hair was loose, drawn back into a tail. Her mouth was full, her nose slightly arched. She was tall and moved deliberately as she approached Ben Flowers.

'That is your name, isn't it?' she asked, as Ben paused before throwing his saddle onto the sorrel's hack. 'Ben Flowers?'

'Yes,' he replied. 'Have we met?'

'No. I need a man to escort me to Pawnee.'

'You can't mean me?'

'Yes.' She leaned against the stall partition, resting her arms on it. 'You see . . . Ben, it's like this. My husband, Tom Cole, is returning from a long cattle drive to Oregon. He wrote me to say that he will meet me in Pawnee where we hope to take up residence.'

She paused. 'The letter took a long time to reach me, and I am very late. I thought there was stagecoach service from Fargo to Pawnee, but there is not, it turns out. I was over at the courthouse to ask the marshal if he could spare a man to ride with me, but he refused. A clerk from the county recorder's office happened to overhear me and he pointed you out, saying that you were riding that way.'

'Not all the way,' Ben Flowers said, tightening his cinches. 'My property' – he liked the sound of that and repeated it – 'my property is about ten miles this side of Pawnee.'

'That's close enough. I'll take my chances from there. But I am fearful of riding the long plains by myself, a woman alone.'

Ben nodded, straightening from his task. He tilted his hat back and told the woman, 'I can see you along the trail that far – if you'll trust me to do it.'

She smiled prettily and answered, 'I trust you. You have kind eyes. If you'll just give me time enough to get into my riding clothes . . . I've already purchased a horse. That little paint pony over there. I can't thank you enough.' She spoke in a rush now, as if she were afraid he might change his mind, ride away and leave her. 'My husband will thank you as well. I can't miss meeting him.' She turned and started away, hoisting her skirt. Pausing briefly, she called back down the stable aisle, 'My name is Elizabeth! Elizabeth Cole.'

'I'll have your pony saddled when you get back,' Ben Flowers said.

As the young blonde flitted out from the intense shadows of the stable into the bright sunlight he wondered why he had agreed to her request so readily. But then, it was not safe for a woman alone out on the Great Plains; too much could go wrong. It was the only decent thing to do. And there were worse fates than having a lovely blonde companion along on his ride *home.*

He went to find the stableman and ask for Elizabeth Cole's tack.

*

The morning was still bright, the skies holding fine though there was a wind rising as they cleared the town limits of Fargo and turned their horses southward toward Pawnee. Elizabeth, wearing a divided buckskin skirt now and a high-necked white blouse, spoke excitedly as they rode – of her husband and their plans for the future. She was eager to reach Pawnee, as eager as Ben Flowers himself. She did make an enjoyable riding companion. The miles they traveled across the long-grass plains passed easily, and she was a delight to study, as cheerful and animated as she was. It certainly made the long ride more pleasant than if he had made the trek alone.

'Can we make Pawnee by nightfall?' Elizabeth asked, late that afternoon as the few high clouds that had begun to drift in from Canada were touched with color on their underbellies. The rising wind shifted her hastily pinned blonde hair across her face and into her eyes. Ben shook his head.

'I don't really know. I only know this land from descriptions and from maps. You know how misleading maps can seem, even if they're well drawn, which they aren't in this part of the country.'

'I know,' Elizabeth answered. 'On a map China is about three inches across.'

Ben grinned. 'Well, that's where we stand. I believe we can make my ranch, but I'm not even sure of that.'

'Are there other people there? Beds? Food?'

Ben smiled again, this time more dourly.

'So far as I know there's nothing there. No one's been on the land for five years. But if we can make it, we'll have a roof over us if it should decide to rain – which,' he said, eyeing the ominously gathering clouds, 'seems likely.'

'I see,' Elizabeth said. It was obvious that she wanted to rush onto Pawnee, but a rainstorm would make that a long, cold, disorienting ride. 'Well, we'll do what we must!' she said with another of her bright smiles. 'Don't sailors say, "any port in a storm"?'

Forty minutes later it began to rain. It was a sudden hard wash of silver, driving down on their hacks, soaking them through in minutes. Both had slipped into their slickers as the first squall swept in, but it was too late to protect them from the numbing cold of the open Great Plains storm. Rain stung their eyes, and squinting into the gathering dusk, Ben believed that he had now lost the trail. They rode on in determined silence. Speech was nearly impossible above the howl of the wind anyway.

Yet, a mile farther on the low clouds parted briefly and through the falling rain Ben saw the low form of a log building. He reined up and sat his sorrel horse for a long minute, staring into the dark, falling rain. Confused, Elizabeth touched his arm and asked, 'What is it, Ben?'

His answer was barely audible above the gusting wind. 'I'm riding on my own land,' he told her eventually. 'The ground below us is mine; that cabin is mine.'

She didn't understand the fervor in his voice, nor did she care at that moment. She only wanted to get to someplace dry and be sheltered against the driving storm.

The cabin was in complete disrepair. Of the riddled front door, half off its leather hinges, Elizabeth remarked. 'Looks like the moths have been at it.'

'Probably someone using it for target practice,' Ben said, his enthusiasm undiminished. It took them long minutes working in the dark to find a pair of candles stored in a cupboard with a tilted door, but the flickering light these offered when lit was welcome. 'There's no wood for the fire, I suppose,' Elizabeth said, her teeth chattering.

'I don't see any. We're sure not going to find anything dry outside to burn. 'We'll have to suffer through it, I guess.'

'So it seems.' Still Elizabeth's good spirits were not dampened. She had made it this far and tomorrow she would be in Pawnee to meet Tom Cole. There were two bunks in a back room, three wooden chairs around a puncheon table, some scattered pots and pans in the tiny kitchen area. Nothing much else. The roof leaked very badly in one corner, not so badly in the others.

'Careful!' Ben warned as Elizabeth crossed the front room, for someone had torn up some of the floorboards. Studying this with puzzlement, Ben said, 'Probably some passerby using them for firewood.'

There wasn't much more to be seen by the flickering light of the candles. The place was obviously a mess, but Ben hadn't expected much more of a cabin that hadn't been occupied for over five years. Morning was soon enough to survey the work he needed to do. For now he stifled a yawn, went to the badly hung front door and closed it.

'Let's get what sleep we can,' he said to Elizabeth. 'We both have busy days tomorrow.'

Ben went into the sleeping nook, looked under a bunk and kicked it with his boot, checking for lurking critters. It seemed safe enough and so he let Elizabeth crawl onto it and close her eyes, still wearing her rain slicker. Ben had opted to try dozing on one of the chairs.

He was too excited to sleep much. He had made it home. Sagging onto the wooden chair, he folded his arms, listened to the rain dripping through the roof and smiled to himself The cabin wouldn't suit everybody, but he had slept in far worse situations on the open trail, and this place, such as it was, was his very own. Sometime before dawn he did actually manage to fall asleep.

Jerking awake, disoriented and stiff, Ben Flowers rubbed his head and rose to his feet. The front door was open. Morning light glistened on the long grass, scattering jewels of dew across the land. The big oak tree in the yard dripped silver droplets. The air was cold but the wind had died down. The skies were clearing with only a few lazy behemoth clouds drilling slowly past.

It was a miserable but glorious morning. The first day.

He glanced toward the sleeping area where Elizabeth had been the night before, but she was gone. Frowning, he looked around and finally found the note scrawled in pencil that she had left hanging on a nail on the wall.

Clear skies. Off to Pawnee. Thanks – Elizabeth Cole

Well, he wished he had had the chance to say goodbye to her, but he could understand her eagerness. Her husband was arriving. Soon they would be starting a new life. As would Ben Flowers.

Rincon was already up and breakfasted when Elizabeth found him in Pawnee's only restaurant. She dropped into the seat across the table from him and gestured to the waitress, miming a poured can of coffee. Rincon did not look much different than when they had sent him up five years ago, but his dark mustache had been shaved and his lips only twitched when he offered a smile. He stretched his hands across the table and took Elizabeth's.

'Missed you,' he said.

'You missed *any* woman,' she said, as the tired-looking waitress brought Elizabeth a mug of steaming coffee.

'Not like I missed you,' Rincon said, as he removed his hands so that the half-frozen Elizabeth could sip at her coffee. She tried very hard to believe his words.

Glancing around the room carefully, he asked in a low voice, 'How did it go?'

'The kid's as dumb as a stump,' Elizabeth answered.

'He doesn't know about the gold, then? When I first heard that the Whittaker property was going up for sale, I wondered.'

'He doesn't know a thing.' Elizabeth said. 'I spent all day with him. He's just a wet-nosed kid all excited about having his own half-section. I grilled him pretty well – without him knowing it of course.'

'Did you have to smile a lot?' Rincon asked coldly.

'Only smile,' Elizabeth said stiffly. 'Look, Rincon, I waited five years for you to be released. Why would I start speculating now?'

'I don't know. I'm sorry,' he said with bland insincerity.

'If you'd been able to send me some money I could have outbid the kid for the property and we could have searched at leisure; but you never—'

'Where was I supposed to get money, locked down in the Territorial Prison?' Rincon said, and then he realized he was speaking too loudly and lowered his voice. 'Anyway, this might turn out just as well. The kid shouldn't be a problem for us.'

'Us?' Elizabeth said. 'Where is Cal Mercer anyway?'

'He got an extra month for slugging a prison guard. Losing that arm has just made him meaner than he ever was.'

'And he was pretty mean before,' Elizabeth commented. She was silently thoughtful as the waitress refilled her coffee cup. When the aproned woman had walked away, Elizabeth leaned forward and asked in a whisper, 'What if we can find where Billy Carter stashed the army gold before Cal Mercer is released from prison? I mean . . . do we still have to cut him in?'

'That,' Rincon said, sipping his own coffee, 'is something we will have to consider carefully, isn't it?'

Ben Flowers had decided to tackle the roof first. His sorrel, picketed out beyond the oak tree grazed placidly on the long grass of the plains. Ben had discovered a ladder in the broken-down lean-to which had once served as a shed and, poking around, a dull saw, a barrelful of rusty nails and a few slats; not enough to do the job, but enough to give him a start. He still had a little pocket money and, after the rough work was done, he planned to ride into Pawnee himself and purchase some decent tools and shingles.

The roughly made pole ladder looked hazardous, and Ben tested it carefully before deciding that it would take his weight. Surprisingly, the ancient contraption allowed him to climb to the roof, a bucketful of nails hitched to his belt, hammer tucked in behind. Then he hefted the stack of slats he had roped together and got them up, losing two or three as they slipped the knot.

The roof was only slightly pitched, but when Ben's boot hit a mossy spot, it was enough to send him into a brief, scrambling slide toward the edge of the roof.

A mocking voice called up, 'What are you doing up there! Or should I say, what are you *trying* to do?'

Sitting, his knees drawn up, Ben looked into the morning sunlight to see a skinny kid on an outsized, hairy buckskin horse in his front yard. The kid wore a wide fawn-colored Stetson, black jeans and a checked red shirt. Scowling, Ben answered, rubbing the elbow he had skinned.

'Patching my roof if you don't mind.'

'Your roof? You mean you actually bought this place?'

'Took it over for taxes,' Ben shouted. He realized that he had lost his grip on the slats and would have to descend the ladder. The kid had swung down from the big-shouldered buckskin horse to watch with evident amusement. Smothering a curse, Ben retraced his path. Reaching the ground he began to bundle the slats again. The kid's shadow fell across him.

'You ought to use some proper roofmg materials.'

'This is all that's at hand,' Ben said rising from his crouch. 'Anyway—' He turned to find himself facing the kid who was at least a head shorter than he was, narrowly built. The Stetson hat had been removed to show a roughly sawn-off crop of black hair which the kid was scratching at vigorously.

'I'm damned,' Ben said. 'You're a girl.'

'I am a woman. My name is Kate McCallister and I am twenty-two years of age. I am slenderly built. People keep telling me that I will fill out, but I hope not. I feel more secure the way I am.'

'I don't get you.'

Kate McCallister shrugged. 'Of course not; you're a man, aren't you?'

Ben didn't know what to say. Eventually he introduced himself. 'I'm Ben Flowers. Why did you sound surprised when I said that this was my place?'

'Oh,' she answered, shrugging one shoulder. 'I just didn't think that anyone would want to live here again.'

'Why not?' Ben asked with surprise. 'What is it, haunted or something?'

'Maybe,' the girl answered. 'Maybe worse. Come with me, I want to show you something.'

Going around to the front of the cabin, Kate pointed to a series of holes bored into the face of the unbarked logs.

'Woodpeckers?' Ben asked in puzzlement.

The girl laughed. 'Sure! I'll show you,' she said, taking a pocket knife from her jeans. Digging into one of the holes she worked at it until she had pried out a misshapen lead slug. She displayed it in the palm of her small hand. 'There's over a hundred of these holes in the front wall, Mr Ben Flowers. You surely noticed the door?'

He had, but he had taken it for careless shooters using the deserted cabin for target practice. He took the slug from her hand and asked, 'What does this mean? What happened here?'

'No one knows for certain except that the army was involved. Father bolted our door and shuttered the windows. We couldn't see anything much, but we could hear the guns firing for nearly an hour.'

'Is that what happened to the last owner?' he asked thoughtfully. 'He was killed?'

'Yes, but there are a lot of other people involved in whatever happened here. You'd better hope they don't come back.'

THREE

'Place is really a mess, isn't it?' Kate McCallister said as they entered the cabin to look it over by daylight. 'Still, I guess it could be fixed up decent if a person had the time and the money.'

'I've plenty of time,' Ben Flowers replied thinly, not bothering to state the obvious problem. He found the previous day's euphoria fading rapidly in the reality of the light of the new morning. The roof was a disaster; the floorboards had been torn up. He would probably be better off burning the mattresses. The kitchen nook was filthy. Rats had been in it, feeding on food hastily left behind. He bent to pick up an old pot that rested on the floor and grimly showed it to Kate. His finger fit neatly into a bullet hole in it.

'All right,' Kate said briskly, as she dusted off

one of the wooden chairs with a kerchief and seated herself at the puncheon table. 'Wipe that gloomy look off your face, Ben Flowers. You knew everything couldn't be done in a day. What are your plans, exactly?'

'I'm afraid they're kind of inexact,' he answered, standing with his back to the scarred stone fireplace. 'I really haven't even had the time to look around yet. The place is in disrepair, that's for sure.'

'Look, Ben, how much did you pay for this place?'

'Five hundred and thirteen dollars.'

'And for that what did you expect?'

'You're right, of course. It's just that I had hopes. . . .'

'Forget hopes and dreams,' she said with a sort of gloomy cheerfulness. 'Now you're going to have to deal with the reality of the situation. So, what are you going to do first, Ben?'

Her eyes, a darker blue than he had thought at first reflected real interest. She held her hands clasped between her knees; the Stetson sat on the table beside her.

'The roof, of course. In case it rains again soon.'

'It will. The storms this time of year always come in clusters.'

'Then,' Ben said with weary determination, 'I have to find the well and dig it out. Floor the cabin, bring in food and firewood, assuming I can locate any dry wood. Then there's the property corner markers, of course. I want to find them so that I can be sure where my land begins and ends.'

'I can help you with that along the southern boundary – that's where Father's land begins. I've seen the markers.'

'That would be a help. Then there's the general clean-up in here, building some sort of shelter for my horse . . . and that's only a start, isn't it? I mean, that's just the structures. Then the real work starts, trying to make something of this land.' Despondency seemed to have settled again.

Kate leaned forward and unexpectedly touched his knee. She smiled and said quietly, 'Even in your dreams you can't have expected to accomplish it all in a single day.' She got to her feet, turning around slowly, surveying the dilapidated structure. 'I do have one suggestion for you, though. After the roof . . . move the front door up on your list. Get that hung right and reinforced as soon as possible.'

'You're still thinking I might have uninvited guests arriving?'

'I don't know, but I'd consider it if I were you. Now then,' Kate went on more brightly, 'you'll have to he going into Pawnee soon for supplies if you're going to get anything done. Stock up on a few basic food supplies and bring back what building materials you can.'

'That will be tough on horseback,' Ben said.

'Father will loan you a buckboard. Today would be the day to go into Pawnee. For tonight at least, it will not rain. The roof can wait that long. I'll talk to my father and see that a wagon is sent over. After all, Ben, we are neighbors and out here and we are all we have to rely on.'

'I thank you – enormously,' he answered. Mentally he was counting his greatly diminished cash money. He was going to have to spend most of it even to get a start on things. And then – where would future income come from? He had no idea, but one day at a time seemed to be the attitude to adopt right now.

'Your father's ranch?' he asked, as he escorted the girl back toward the front door.

'What is it called?'

She laughed. 'The McCallister Place, I suppose.'

'I thought maybe you had a brand.'

She shook her head. 'We have a few cattle, mostly for our own use. We have some horses, but Father never got around to registering a brand. We know them all by sight anyway.'

'Does he have any stock he might consider selling?' Ben asked.

'I don't know.' Her eyes were enquiring, have you any money you could buy steers with? 'I'll ask him.'

The wind was brisk but not unpleasant outside. Kate swung easily onto the back of her outsized, hairy buckskin horse, surveyed the house again and said, 'You've got your work cut out for you. We'll try to find someone to help you out from time to time.

'Ben,' she asked, leaning down slightly, 'the house, the condition it's in – is that the reason your woman wouldn't stay?'

'My—?'

'The blonde woman. We saw her early this morning. She was cutting across our ranch, trying to find the way to Pawnee.'

'Oh. That was Elizabeth Cole. Just someone I met along the way. She's on her way to meet her husband.'

Kate planted her broad Stetson on her head, turned her horse southward and waved good-bye, an elfin smile passing over her lips. *Now what was that about?*

Shaking his head, Ben went out to move his sorrel's picket pin. The leggy horse had mowed most of the grass nearby. After that, having given up on roofing until he could obtain the proper materials, he surveyed the area nearest the house. He found the old well, boarded over with soggy, mossy boards, slid a few aside and tried to estimate how much labor would be involved in cleaning it out. Years of mud and slime must have accumulated there. At least he had a well. When summer came it would be a matter of importance. For now there was plenty of available water in a quick-flowing rill not far from the back of the house where a stand of green willow trees and a sycamore or two grew.

Ben tried the rusty windlass over the well and found it frozen with rust, but, with a surge of effort, he managed to break the corroded gears free. Squeaking and complaining with years of neglect, the crank nevertheless turned. A little oil might solve that without much trouble. He wound the ancient rope up around the windlass spool, hoping that there was still a bucket on the bottom. That might be a help in cleaning out the well. There was no such luck. The rope, rotted away after years in the slime came up frayed and rank, no bucket to be seen. Well, why should he have expected that one might be? Slogging up and down a ladder all day with bucketsful of mud and debris from the well was going to be a tedious, exhausting job. With two men, one in the well shoveling, the other drawing the muck up, things would go much quicker. Kate had said something about them possibly loaning him a man for a few days, so maybe that was a plan to be considered. He put a bucket, new rope and machine oil on his mental list of things that needed to be purchased and went on with his inspection of the property, wiping his hands on his blue jeans.

The lean-to where horses had been stabled at one time, judging by the pungency of the place, was in disrepair. Half of the roof had fallen in, but he thought that it was basically sound and could be put back in order with a day or two's work.

Hungry now, he returned to the cabin and dug through his saddle-bags for the little food he had on hand – a few salt biscuits and some venison jerky. By the time he had finished his poor meal he could hear the creaking of a wagon's wheels, the steady clomping of horses' hoofs. Approaching the door cautiously, he peered out to see Kate McCallister sitting the spring seat of a buckboard. She waved a gauntleted hand at him.

'If we're going to make Pawnee and get back by nightfall, we'd better be moving!' she called.

Puzzled, Ben grabbed his rifle from inside the cabin and walked to the wagon parked in the shade of the wide-spreading oak tree.

'I know that you said that your father might lend me a wagon,' Ben said, looking up at Kate McCallister, 'but I didn't expect you to deliver it. What are we going to do? Drop you off at your father's ranch?'

'Oh, no!' Kate laughed. 'I'm a part of the deal. I'm driving. Father doesn't mind helping a neighbor, but he's not going to lend a good wagon and team of horses to a man he's never even met.'

'He's a cautious man,' Ben said, climbing

aboard to seat himself beside Kate.

'He is, and it's served him well. He's survived this long out on the plains.' Kate started the team forward and smiled at Ben. 'We've only two ranch hands and they're both busy. I wanted to go into town to get a few things for myself anyway.' They exited the dappled shade of the oak and drove out into the clear, cool sunlight, Kate guiding the team of matched bays expertly. There was something different about her and it took Ben a while to puzzle it out. As the buckboard jounced along the rough road he suddenly figured what it was. There was a faint scent of jasmine around them which came from no growing flowers. Again Kate glanced at him, smiled and turned her eyes away.

The road now began to follow a willow-lined creek, glinting silver in the sunlight. A few minutes on, Kate reined up and pointed at a small pile of white-painted stones. 'That's your south-west corner marker. You should be able to find the other corners with your map if you start from there.'

'I think I can. Thank you.'

She shrugged as if it were nothing and started the team forward again.

'Does that mean we're on your father's ranch now?' he asked.

'Over there,' she said, pointing to their left. 'You should just be able to make out our house on that knoll.'

Ben looked that way, but could not see it. He did notice a few cattle, and a dozen or so horses as they passed. There was a stock pen as well, and inside it, his boot propped on the lowest rail, was a glowering man in a denim jacket, his hat lifted back, eyeing them closely as the buckboard clattered past.

'That was one tough-looking man,' Ben said, frowning.

'That,' she replied, 'was my father.'

The day rolled past beneath the wheels of the wagon. There were teal ducks along the creek, paddling one way and then the other in unison. and doves flying across the silver-blue sky.

'Who owned my property before I did?' Ben enquired. 'I'm still trying to figure out what sort of trouble I might expect.'

Kate's blue eyes became briefly intent. Her Stetson hat had flipped back to ride on her back on its drawstring and her short black hair was ruffled by the passing breeze.

'The Whittaker brothers,' she answered finally. 'There were six of them, all filthy and mean. None of them would have known what a razor was for if he ever came across one. Or soap, for that matter. Two of them stayed pretty much to home: Deuce and Jacob. I don't know the names of all the rest of them, though I think one was called Ned, one Barstow – my father might know – but we always kept well shy of those Whittaker brothers.'

'Only two of them stayed at the house?'

'The two that were killed there,' Kate said. 'Watch it – we've got a rough crossing coming up,' and she slowed the team to let it find its way across a rocky fork of the broad, shallow creek. When the horses had picked their way across the ford, she went on with her story.

'Deuce and Jacob were killed in that cabin. Some think the army shot them down, but the whole story never came out.'

'And the other brothers?' Ben asked.

'No one knows. They were never around much anyway. Some people said that they went out robbing and only came back to the ranch when they needed a place to hide out. I don't think anyone knows for sure.'

'After five years . . . if they were alive and wanted the property, surely they would have laid claim to it.'

'It could be either way, I guess,' Kate said, as they approached the town of Pawnee. 'Either they are all dead or they plain didn't care to have to do the work to maintain a house they never lived in. Nevertheless, Ben,' she added seriously, 'keep an eye open. Who knows when one or all of them could take a notion to return. They might figure that the property still belongs to them no matter what the law says.'

'That's him!' Elizabeth Cole said, grabbing Rincon's arm as the wagon made its way up Pawnee's dusty main street toward the hardware store at the south end of town.

'Who's what?' Rincon said, jerking his arm free with annoyance. Elizabeth turned him to face her on the awning-shaded plankwalk in front of the hotel.

'Him!' she said, jabbing a finger in the direction of the wagon. 'That's Benjamin Flowers, the kid who bought the Whittaker place.'

'Are you sure?' Rincon asked, frowning as he squinted into the bright sunlight.

'I just fmished riding all the way from Fargo with him, didn't I? Of course I'm sure. That's Ben Flowers.'

'Who's the girl?'

'I have no idea.' Elizabeth took his arm again. 'Rincon, wouldn't this be a good time to search the ranch – while he's busy here?'

'There wouldn't be enough time. It's going to take a lot of looking. That damned Billy . . . why did he have to get himself killed out there?'

Because Billy Carter, wherever he had hidden the army gold, had done a good job of it. Off and on some of the locals who had heard the rumors and, Rincon guessed, some of the soldiers who had been involved in the chase, had returned to the Whittaker place and torn it apart looking for the stash. No, it would take more than blind determination. It would take careful thought to recover the gold, to figure out where Billy could have hidden it in the little time that he had had to do it on that night.

With the land and cabin abandoned, Rincon had figured that he would have all the time he needed to puzzle it out, but now this Ben Flowers was in the way.

Rincon had not spent five years in prison to give up on that hidden fortune now.

Ben Flowers's purse was much lighter, but the buckboard was heavier, laden with lumber, hardware and foodstuffs as they rolled out of town. On the seat between them was a small packet of dainties Kate had bought for herself as Ben made his purchases, working a balancing act between what he knew he needed and thought he could afford. In the end he believed that he had done all right. Sawn wood, of course, was at a premium out on the long plains, but there was some surplus lumber left over from the new Pawnee stage station stacked in the back yard of the store which they had let him have at a discount.

As they made their way homeward, dusk began to settle. Already the frogs were grumbling along the creek and the night birds had begun to fly. The sky was cloudless but for a low fortress-like formation far to the north. These would creep in slowly but surely, and Ben could only hope that the heavy rains held off until he was able to patch his roof properly.

No matter, for today he was content. He had

shingles, planks to patch his torn-up cabin floor and even a bundle of oak firewood purchased from a vendor with a wagonful of the stuff they had passed along the main street.

'Feeling better now?' Kate asked, as she guided the team along the narrow trail.

'Better, but much poorer.'

'Well,' she said, 'you couldn't just go on looking at the place wishing that something could be done.'

'No,' he admitted. 'I thank you – and your father – for helping me out.'

'That's what neighbors are for,' Kate said with a brief smile.

They were crossing the creek when the rifle shots rang out, breaking the sundown silence.

The first shot was far too close, splatting against the side of the buckboard. 'Whip 'em!' Ben shouted, but Kate McCallister was already yelling at the horses, snapping the reins to urge them on.

Ben Flowers crawled from the bench seat and over onto the stack of lumber and burlap bags in the bed of the wagon and began opening up with his Winchester as he caught the winking eye of a muzzle flash in the willows across the stream. Prone, he continued to fire at his target, burning up ammunition as the jolting wagon reached the trail on the far side of the creek and raced on.

'Get him?' Kate shouted across her shoulder.

'It'd be a miracle if I did,' Ben answered. Warily he eased his way back into his seat on the wagon bench. 'I wonder what that was about,' he said, his throat dry with the aftermath of excitement.

'Well,' Kate said, slowing the team as they came within sight of the McCallister place, 'I doubt they wanted to kill me. I don't think there's enough in this wagon to warrant armed robbery. We have to conclude that someone wants to kill you, Ben Flowers.'

FOUR

It was nearly full dark before they had managed to unload the wagon. The lumber sat in neat stacks to one side of the house, the foodstuffs had been taken inside. Kate, miniature woman that she appeared to be, was strong and eagerly helpful. Before Ben had finished taking his sorrel to the rill, watered it and again picketed it out on new grass, the girl had started a fire in the stone fireplace and had coffee boiling. She had taken off her boots and sat in one of the wooden chairs, her head tilted back, eyes half closed.

'Where'd you get the water?' he asked.

'From my canteen. Coffee should be ready in another ten minutes.'

'Chimney should have been checked out

before you started that fire.'

'I did. Good God, Ben, do you take me for some city woman?'

'No. It's just that I've never met a woman so willing to share the load.'

She laughed. 'There's lots of us, Ben! It seems you just haven't met too many women.'

That was true, he reflected. A cowhand on the trail, a man lumberjacking in the far north woods, wasn't likely to have the chance to meet many women. He fell silent. After a few minutes he poured them each a cup of the freshly boiled coffee and pulled another chair up beside Kate. They watched the twisting gold and crimson flames in the fireplace in companionable silence for a while.

Eventually Kate asked, 'You didn't get a look at the man who was shooting, did you?'

'Not even a shadow.' He had seen a horse, or imagined he had. But it made no sense for that animal to be there. It might have been his imagination, must have been.

Because he thought that he had glimpsed beyond the screen of willow brush a little paint pony just like the one Elizabeth Cole had ridden.

'Who do you think it was?' Ben asked, after another minute which he had spent watching the black-haired tomboy sipping her coffee from a tin cup. 'The Whittaker brothers?'

'No,' Kate said with a shake of her head. 'You don't know them. Their way would be just to ride in, bust down the door and tell you to get out or get shot.'

'Who then. . . ?' He rose and tossed the dregs of his coffee into the fire where they hissed and spat. 'I haven't been here long enough to make any enemies.'

'Ben,' Kate said, tugging on her boots, 'I think that unknowingly you made enemies when you bought this ranch.'

'So it seems,' he answered darkly. He glanced toward the open door. The sky was deep purple. Night was settling rapidly. 'It's close to nightfall. Your father will be wondering what's happened to you.'

'He'll be wondering what happened to his horses and the buckboard,' Kate laughed. 'I'm on my way. Ben,' she said, putting on her Stetson. 'I'll try to see about getting you some help over here tomorrow.'

'Thank you, Kate. You've already been a big

help. Really.'

'I try,' she said, and then she strolled toward the door, her boyish figure trim and somehow attractive in the firelight. She waved a hand in parting and then started the team homeward. Ben watched her until he could no longer see the buckboard in the falling darkness. Then he went back into the cabin, closed the door and watched the dying flames in the fireplace for a long while.

When he could no longer hold his eyes open he dragged himself onto one of the cots and stretched out, his Colt revolver near at hand, and stared at the ceiling, thinking that the house now seemed colder . . . and much emptier.

'I take it that you didn't get him,' Elizabeth Cole said, as a glowering Rincon tramped into the hotel room they shared and threw his saddle across the room.

'No, damnit! But the kid almost got me. I thought you said he was green.'

'I said he was green, not that he couldn't shoot.'

Rincon sagged onto the bed and Elizabeth, in her pinafore, sat beside him, her hand briefly stroking his head.

'So what do we do now?'

'Be patient, I guess,' Rincon responded.

'I thought you said we couldn't wait too long. What if Cal Mercer shows up and we still haven't found the gold? He'll claim half of it you know.'

'I know that,' Rincon said. He rose, went to the washstand, dipped his hands into the bowl and wiped his hands across his hair. 'I can control Cal Mercer. I've done it before.'

'And if you can't? You said yourself that he's gotten even wilder since that soldier shot his arm off. Five years in prison can't have made him less crazy.'

'I said I could handle Mercer!' Rincon said loudly. He turned to face the lovely blonde woman, her hair loose around her shoulders.

'What about those Whittaker brothers? What if they come back, Rincon? They'll run the kid off the land, won't they?'

'No one's even seen them for years. They are all scattered, dead or locked up somewhere. Besides, they know nothing about the gold.'

'As far as you know,' Elizabeth said. 'It seems to be pretty much common knowledge around Pawnee.'

'We'll deal with them if it ever comes up – which I don't expect will happen.'

'One thing they are bound to know,' Elizabeth said, rising to stand beside her man, 'is that Cal Mercer killed at least one of their brothers.'

'I know,' Rincon said, going to the window to look out across the small town, the long plains beyond. 'Makes it complicated, doesn't it? We have to get this done before anyone else shows up.'

'Was any of it worth it?' Elizabeth asked, as she stood beside Rincon, her arm looped around him.

'It was. Still is,' he answered. 'I have five years of my life invested in it now. And twenty-thousand gold dollars is just about enough to make it up to me. The only thing I regret is pulling that dumb soldier, Billy Carter, into the job.'

'Using the company clerk was the only way to do the job, Rincon. What else were you going to do, crash into the fort and blow up the safe?'

'In the end,' Rincon answered, 'that might have been simpler.'

Ben Flowers was up with the sun. It took him

only two hours to patch the lean-to together so that it was a reasonable shelter for his horse and he led the sorrel there and filled its water trough with water from the flowing rill behind the house. The well would be a convenience, but surveying the iob had convinced him that cleaning it out was at least a day or two-day chore for two men. He glanced at the skies where thunderheads were building, but they seemed to stand motionless. The roof needed to be patched, but he shrugged off that difficult task in favor of the simpler job of replacing the floorboards in the cabin.

It all had to be done and the order of repairs wasn't that important. Anyone not noticing the missing floorboards could easily break a leg. He went to the wood stack, and carried the new planks inside. Measuring, he sawed the boards on the front porch, nailing them down with a new hammer he had purchased. The ringing sounds of nails being pounded, the purr of the saw blade cutting through fresh lumber, were somehow soothing – something was being done. His dream, distant as it might be, was beginning to take form.

Stepping away from his work to study the

floorboards, he stood hands on hips, wondering again why they had been torn up. It was as if someone had been searching for something. For what?

'That's an improvement,' the voice from the doorway said, and he turned with a smile to find that Kate McCallister had arrived, unheard.

'Well, it's something,' he answered. 'Did you notice the lean-to?'

'Sure did. I put old Buck in there to have a horse-conversation with your sorrel.'

'I don't know how much more I can do today,' Ben said, seating himself in one of the chairs. 'Most everything else I have planned will take at least a full day, and I'm beat.' He asked, 'I guess you weren't able to find a helper for me.'

'He's here,' Kate said, 'and he is me. Our two ranch hands are very busy, and I don't have a lot to do. I like feeling useful. Go on ahead doing whatever you have in mind. I'll try to set that rat-trap of a kitchen right. Did you remember to buy paint like I told you?'

And they got to work again. They paused briefly for lunch at one in the afternoon. It wasn't much – beans, sausage and apples, but it was something to sustain them and, as they ate facing each other across the puncheon table, it seemed a fine feast to Ben Flowers.

By evening Ben had torn off the old door and replaced it with one with sturdy new inch-thick planks, hung now on iron hinges. Inside the house the smell of new paint was evident. Going that way, Ben was surprised to see the pantries laden, the doors to the cupboards hung, everything fresh and glossy with white paint.

'You are a marvel,' he said to Kate who turned toward him, white paint flecking her dark hair, smudging her nose.

'This,' she said, waving a negligent hand, 'this is nothing! You ought to see me when I really get my teeth into a job.'

'I'd hate to think what you could do in weeks, months!' he said admiringly.

'You can't even imagine what I could do in years,' he heard Kate say before she scooped up an empty can of white paint, brushed past him and went out the newly hung door.

And what did she mean by that? Ben wondered, as he watched her slender back fade into silhouette before the magnificent colors of the sundown sky. The girl was a mystery. He went out onto the porch in time to see her guiding her shaggy buckskin horse homeward. He called and lifted a hand, but got no response. Yes, he decided, the girl was a mystery.

Ben pulled off his boots and set water boiling in the black iron pot in the fireplace. He was tired and smelled of salt. He needed to wash up and then . . . and then what? It was far too early to go to sleep, and the cabin, improved as it was, was still somehow depressingly lacking. Washing up with a cloth as the fire burned low he decided on a course of action.

He should, out of common courtesy ride to the McCallister place and formally introduce himself to Kate's father. After all, the man had helped him with the loan of buckboard and team, without which his efforts at improving the property would not have progressed this far. Too, he could enquire into the possibility of buying a few steers, perhaps a second horse. It might be that McCallister had seed-corn to spare, even a plow he might be willing to lend or sell.

These, he decided, were enough reasons to go to Kate's father's house, and so he dug out a fresh blue shirt from his kit, donned it and went to saddle the sorrel while there was still light in the skies.

The white house was much larger than Ben Flowers had expected. Two wings spread out from the plantation-style center with its four columns. It was plain that McCallister was here to stay. Light glowed from within, spilling out through the two arched windows. Ben's arrival brought two wary men, roughly dressed, into the yard sheltered by a dozen tall elms, their branches spreading lacy star-shadows across the yard.

'You have business here?' the taller of the two men asked. He took the bridle to Ben's sorrel without instruction and held it firmly.

'Just a neighborly visit,' Ben said uneasily. 'I'm Ben Flowers; I just bought the old Whittaker place.'

'He's all right, Hugh,' the second ranch hand said. 'He's the one that's been sparking Miss Kate.'

Sparking? This was hardly the time to set the men straight, since the bigger man – Hugh – still stood holding his horse's bridle, his hand poised near the gun on his hip, and so Ben just smiled uneasily and swung down.

'Where can I tie up my horse?' he asked.

'We'll take care of that for you, friend,' Hugh answered. 'Just go on in.'

The two, whoever they were, were watchful and obviously loyal. It reminded Ben of the cowhands he had worked with down in Texas, men who rode for the brand and had in effect sworn allegiance to it.

The front door was painted white and had brass fittings. It was intimidating in its way, but it stood slightly open. He knocked lightly and went in as he had been instructed. The man he came face to face with was much more intimidating than any door. Standing in the vestibule wearing a gray suit and vest was Kate's father. He had his hands behind his back. His eyebrows were folded together in study. His hair was as shortly cropped as a Prussian officer's, his jawline was broad and firm. Clean-shaven and tanned, he looked a hybrid between East and West. There was no mistaking his authority.

'I'm Abel McCallister. You must be Flowers,' he said extending a hand. 'I've been expecting you.'

Despite his military appearance and intimidating demeanor, his voice was softly modulated, brisk but not cool. Behind him in the shadows of the large white-painted hall Ben saw Kate. She was wearing a white dress with a blue ribbon woven into the lace of the bodice. Her hair was brushed to a gloss and pinned back from her small ears. Her dark blue eyes seemed wide and apprehensive. She disappeared wraith-like as her father put his arm around Ben's shoulder familiarly and guided him into the room beyond.

'I hope you can stay for supper. We don't have much to offer this evening: duck, ham, sweet potatoes and biscuits, Kate tells me. After we eat we will have time to talk. It appears we have much to talk about.'

The new stage station was the pride of Pawnee, Dakota Territory, if such a scramble-down, ramshackle collection of sorry buildings grouped loosely together, isolated on the plains could even be considered a community, let alone possessed of civic pride. Still, it meant that they had lasted long enough as a pioneering village that they were now connected to the outside world, recognized as being established enough so that the Overland Stage station, newly constructed, offered timetables and issued tickets to the few departing, the few arriving passengers. There was talk of a connecting line to Fargo, but these plans had been suspended for months because of an Indian uprising.

On this velvet-purple evening, the last stage of the day, the week, did arrive in front of the depot of green lumber, still unpainted – squat and small as an orphan pup expecting the worst.

The one-armed man swung down heavily and looked up and down the dusty main street of Pawnee.

'Help with your bags, sir?' an eager attendant in a round black cap asked.

'Got none. Where's the hotel?' Calvin Mercer said.

FIVE

'Now what are we going to do?' Elizabeth Cole whispered to Rincon. Her eyes were frantic as she glanced toward the room adjoining theirs where Calvin Mercer had taken up residence.

'Play the cards that were dealt to us,' Rincon said deliberately. 'We'll have to find a way to use Cal, that's all.'

Elizabeth shook her head. The big one-armed man gave her the shudders. He was a keg of gunpowder waiting to explode. 'He'll want his cut,' Elizabeth whispered. 'It was five years of his life wasted as well.'

'What he wants and what he gets are two different things,' Rincon said, taking Elizabeth's shoulders firmly. 'Meanwhile, he's here and there's nothing we can do about that. You forget, I've known Mercer long and known him well. I can handle him.'

'I hope so, Rincon,' Elizabeth said, her eyes searching his. 'Because he scares the hell out of me, and he should frighten you as well.'

'When did I say he didn't?' Rincon replied evenly. It was true. Even though they had ridden the outlaw trail together, been locked down in the Territorial Prison for five long years, Calvin Mercer was always one step away from crossing the line. He was erratic and plain mean.

And very sudden when it came to killing.

The knock on the door of their room caused their hands to fall away from each other and with a wry smile, Rincon went to answer the door. It was Mercer.

'Now you're looking like a free man,' Rincon said with forced joviality, as Mercer, the trail grime washed away, outfitted in a new pair of black jeans and white shirt Rincon had purchased for him, entered.

'Did you get me a six-gun?' Cal Mercer asked, glancing expressionlessly at Elizabeth, who had withdrawn into the corner near the window.

'The gunshop was closed. We'll take care of that in the morning.'

'And I'll need a horse,' Mercer said, lowering himself clumsily into a chair that seemed too fragile for his bulk. He rubbed his armless shoulder. 'Or do I have to steal one?'

'No. Don't get too hasty, Cal. Neither of us is ready to go back to prison yet.'

'They'll never take me alive,' Mercer swore. 'If that trooper hadn't shot my arm last time. . . .' His bearlike face dropped into a deep frown. 'Where's the damned gold, Rincon?'

'We figure—' Rincon began, but he was interrupted by Mercer.

'I'm not a patient man,' Mercer said, leaning forward like an animal ready to lunge. 'I never was and the last five years have taken away all the patience I might have ever had.'

'I know you are a sudden man,' Rincon said soothingly. 'It's just that we figure it's going to take a little time, so that we don't make a mistake like we did last time.'

Mercer was not mollified, judging by his expression. Rincon took another tack. 'I thought they had given you another thirty days, Cal. How did you get out?'

'I think they just got tired of messing with me,' Mercer said with dark satisfaction. There might have been something implicit in his words, but it was hard to tell with Calvin Mercer. Rincon tried one more diversion.

'What say you and I go out and find ourselves a place to drink, Cal? Elizabeth has a few female things she would like to attend to.'

Mercer looked again at Elizabeth, studying her as if she were a stain on the wall, then he nodded and levered himself up out of the chair. Rincon caught Elizabeth's look of concern behind Cal's back and made a brief, 'What else is there to do?' grimace. Then the two men stamped out of the room, leaving Elizabeth Cole to stand at the open window, looking down at the poor Great Plains town, at the cold sky beyond, wondering what she was doing there. Love or money, she told herself but which? She had thought once that Rincon loved her, but everything seemed to have changed since his release from prison. He was different. He did not touch her, or say sweet things. He had changed, or she, or both of them. As for the money? With Calvin Mercer back in the mix, she would be lucky if she ever saw a single penny of it. She closed the window, sat on the bed and pondered.

It could be a damned hard world.

By midnight when the two men came roistering in with all evidence of comradeship, Elizabeth had been asleep for two hours. Now she covered her head with her pillow and listened without interest to the tales of the old trails Rincon and Mercer had ridden together. They had a whiskey bottle between them on the small hotel room table and sipped at it. Elizabeth knew what Rincon was doing. To protect himself – them – from Cal Mercer's craziness he was bolstering the belief that they were still the best of friends, had always been and would remain so.

It was nearly two in the morning before Mercer, boisterous and staggering, made his way out of the room and went to find his own bed. Elizabeth felt the bed sag as Rincon sat on the foot of the mattress.

'Well?' she asked.

'Well, I was wrong. I don't think I'll be able to control him. I think he's mad now, if he wasn't before.'

'Come to bed, Rincon. There's nothing to be done about it now.'

'No, no there isn't. I just have the feeling that

if someone else doesn't kill him, the job might be left for me to do. He'll ruin everything.'

Elizabeth heard the heavy sound of Rincon's boots falling to the floor as he began to undress. Then she heard a muffled oath, one more violent than she had heard in all of her life.

'What is it Rincon?' she asked, sitting up in bed.

'He couldn't wait until morning,' he answered. Standing near the wooden chair where his gunbelt had hung he told her, 'The bastard took my Colt.'

Ben Flowers slept uneasily. There was too much going on around him that he did not fully understand. Who was the rifleman who had ambushed them earlier in the day? Why? It was unsettling to know that an unknown enemy might be out there, tracking him in his rifle sights each day as he tried to work to improve the small ranch, What chance would he have against a hidden sniper as he, for example, patched the leaky roof? His dream of independence had brought with it an intangible but quite real threat of death. Independence, it seemed, did not ensure freedom.

Beyond all of that there was the question of Kate McCallister. She still remained a mystery. She had said nothing, indicated nothing, but it seemed that not only the ranch hands, but Abel McCallister believed that there was something between Ben and Kate. Ludicrous, really – it would be years before Ben could even consider the idea of supporting a wife.

But, sitting over cigars and brandy in McCallister's den after dinner, the old man had indicated, or at least hinted at the possibility of marriage. McCallister had been agreeable to almost every request Ben had made of him. A horse, a plow, seed – all were graciously granted. As the evening progressed, the reality of the situation had begun to dawn on him. McCallister was granting him more than neighborly assistance. By then, of course, it was too late to back away from the offers.

What, Ben wondered, had Kate told her father? What sort of scheme was she planning? What encouragement had he given her unintentionally?

And – did he really wish to cool her efforts?

He rolled over on the bunk and tried to find a new position more conducive to sleep. The banging at the door was thunderous.

Dressed only in his jeans, Ben rolled from the cot and grabbed for his Colt revolver. No sooner had he wrapped his hand around the walnut grips of the pistol than three shots from without slammed against the newly hung door. The slugs penetrated and Ben threw himself to one side of the room. Rising to a kneeling position he fired five answering shots at the door. He heard a man howl, heard boot steps rushing from the porch and he walked unsteadily toward the door.

Ben snatched up his Winchester which had been leaning in the corner and, taking three deep breaths, he flung open the damaged door. He saw an indistinguishable figure on a shadowy horse riding away from his yard to disappear into the vagueness of the night. He shouldered his rifle, changed his mind and lowered it again.

There was no point in shooting at fast-fleeing ghosts.

Re-entering the cabin he lit a candle and studied the newly made made door. It was splintered, riddled with bullet holes. It had survived all of one day.

How long, Ben wondered, could he survive?

He guessed it was three or four in the morning, but he was far too excited now to go back to what had been an unsatisfactory rest to begin with. He lit two more candles on the mantel and started a small fire. He would sit up, drinking coffee until dawn. Who knew when they – he? – might return?

And who were they, or he? Ben had seen but a single man, but there might have been more hiding in the shadows. The infamous Whittaker brothers came to mind. He knew nothing about them except that they had a wild reputation. A rap at the door brought his head around and caused him to bring up the Colt in his hand. He inched that way cautiously.

'Flowers!' someone called out.

'Who is it?'

'Hugh. We couldn't catch him, but we'll keep our eyes open.'

Hugh? As tautly stretched as his nerves were, it took Ben a moment to remember the tall cowboy from the McCallister place. And what was he doing out there? Cautiously, his Colt held at his side, Ben opened the door.

'Want a cup of coffee?' he asked. 'I've got

some boiling.'

'I wouldn't mind,' the rough-looking cowhand answered, and he tramped in, holding a Winchester rifle loosely in one hand. 'It's been a long night.'

Hugh lowered himself into one of the wooden chairs. He placed his rifle on the table and looked around. 'Well, you've got yourself a start, Flowers. I was by here a month ago and it looked like the place should be burned down and plowed under.'

Ben brought two tin cups of coffee to the table and sat down opposite Hugh. 'Mind if I ask what you were doing out there tonight?'

'Just watching out for you a little. When the boss found out that someone had been shooting at you and his daughter, he was mad as hell. He sent us over to sort of ride lookout. Me and Dusty, that is. You met him last night.'

'I wish Kate hadn't asked him to do that.' Ben said. His mood was sour, the coffee was bitter in the predawn.

'It wasn't her doing,' Hugh said, smiling for the first time since Ben had known him. 'It was McCallister's idea. Mad at the idea of someone shooting at her – or at her man.'

'I'm not her man,' Ben said stiffly.

'Well,' Hugh shrugged, 'time will tell about that. You could do a lot worse than that girl – besides that's McCallister's notion too, not Kate's.'

'I appreciate you boys coming around,' Ben said, turning his cup in his hands, 'but I don't need you here. I really need no help.'

'That's what we all say,' Hugh replied, finishing his coffee, 'but, Flowers, it's wrong. We all need help from time to time. Taking what you can when it's offered is no shame.'

Hugh had been long gone by the time Ben finished his third cup of coffee and began thinking about breakfast. The sky was paling in the east and soon a flourish of crimson and deep violet sprayed itself against the long plains. The hovering clouds were gilded and splashed with crimson, the quick-flowing rill behind the cabin appeared like quicksilver. Ben went out to see to the sorrel horse and to begin to plan his day's work.

The bullet had tagged Cal Mercer high on the thigh. It hurt like hell, but the plank door had slowed the slug down. No artery or bone had been hit. He grimaced with pain as he trailed back into Pawnee. He hoped they had a doctor in this one-horse town.

He was angry and regretful at once. Rincon had told him to be patient, to hold off. He should have listened to him. The man had a cooler head, and that was why they had always made a good team. Rincon thinking things through, and when the time came for action, Calvin bulling in.

How was he going to explain this to Rincon?

Sullenly he rode on, dragging down the main street as the sun rose at his back.

The sun had been up for two hours before Kate McCallister arrived at the ranch on her shaggy buckskin horse. She sprang from the saddle, loosened the horse's cinches and walked toward the cabin. She found Ben Flowers at work on the door.

'I thought you finished that yesterday,' Kate said, stepping up onto the porch.

'It seems it's going to be harder than I thought to get things straightened out around here,' he growled. Rising, he toed his toolbox aside and stretched his back.

'You had trouble, then?'

'Some,' Ben answered, opening and shutting the door to test it. 'Thanks for sending over the bodyguards.'

'I don't know what you mean,' Kate said, to the dour-faced Ben Flowers.

'Hugh and . . . Dusty – that's his name, isn't it?'

'Yes,' Kate answered hesitantly, tilting back her Stetson, allowing it to slip down her back on its tether. 'They were over here? Why? And why do you seem angry about it?'

'I need a cup of coffee,' Ben responded. 'Want some?'

They traipsed into the newly floored cabin and Ben poured as Kate seated herself at the plank table. Ben sailed his hat toward the corner chair. It missed and fell to the floor. Sliding himself into the chair opposite Kate he said, 'Hugh told me that your father sent them over after you said something about the ambush on the trail.'

'Oh?' she said without surprise. 'That's Father. He wouldn't want anything more happening.'

'To you? Or to me?'

Kate's deep blue eyes narrowed questioningly. 'To either of us, I suppose.'

'Hugh also seems to have the idea that you and I are . . . sparking.'

'Does he?'

'Is that the reason that your father is trying to protect me, willing to loan me whatever I might need? Where would he get an idea like that, Kate?'

Rising anger brought hot red spots to her cheeks. 'Not from me!'

'Good, because you know I'm in no position to . . . if I cared to. . . .'

'I accept your apology,' Kate said, her usual good spirits returning. 'Now then – what are we going to work on today?'

Ben frowned, smiled, shrugged and gave it up. She was a mystery. 'The roof, I expect,' he answered eventually.

'Well then, let's get to it. No sense in wasting daylight.'

'Now what are you going to do about him!' Elizabeth Cole demanded, hovering over Rincon who still lay half-asleep in the rumpled bed, sunlight through the hotel window patching the floor. He grumbled something and turned his face into the pillow. Elizabeth, hands on hips, still dressed only in her camisole, let out an exasperated breath.

'You know Calvin dragged himself in here before dawn, shot up! They had to send a doctor up to his room. I heard it all – I wasn't out drinking whiskey half the night.'

'He took a notion,' Rincon said, his voice muffled by the pillow. 'You know Cal.'

'No, I don't, but you're supposed to.' She sat on the bed and placed a hand on his hip. 'You are supposed to be taking care of things, Rincon. To take care of us! Calvin Mercer is – what do the sailors say? – a loose cannon, and he's going to ruin everything.'

'You quote sailors a lot,' Rincon said, sitting up in bed. 'Have you known a few?' He scratched at his downy chest and growled, 'See if we still have any of that whiskey we brought back with us. I feel like hell.'

Elizabeth's mouth grew tight. 'I've never known any sailors, but they are probably better company than drunken gunmen.'

'That wasn't called for, lady,' Rincon said, swinging his legs to the side of the bed as

Elizabeth prowled the room, seeing if the men had indeed failed to finish the whiskey they had brought back from the saloon the previous night.

'I can't find any,' Elizabeth said, after a flurry of opening and slamming drawers shut again. 'I'll go out and get you some if you promise me—' She went to the bedside and knelt in front of Rincon, her hands on his thighs. 'If you promise me that you'll find a way to get rid of Cal Mercer.'

'One thing at a time,' Rincon said, rising to his feet. 'I need a bottle of whiskey to think on.'

And then, as Elizabeth hurriedly dressed in her blue gingham dress and stamped out muttering small feminine curses, Rincon did ponder the situation.

Cal Mercer had jumped the gun again and gotten himself shot up, bringing attention to them all. Would he act any differently given another chance? There was no reason to think so. Now the new owner of the Whittaker ranch was alerted, and chances of jumping him were halved.

As was the gold. Halved. Rincon had believed that he had a month to solve the situation before Mercer was released from prison. Would he have run out afterward and left Cal? Certainly. Now Rincon could only hope for half of the twenty thousand. And what if Calvin Mercer decided that their friendship was not worth that much? Could anyone ever trust Mercer with a gun in his hand? Rincon couldn't: Cal Mercer was a sudden man.

The sun was bright through the window, the morning breeze fluttered the white curtains as Rincon slowly dressed, slowly pondered. Elizabeth was right he would have to get rid of Mercer one way or the other.

Thinking along those lines as he buttoned and tucked in his dark-red shirt, Rincon began to ask himself: what about Elizabeth? Of what use was she beyond the obvious? She would demand her cut of the gold as well, and what had she ever done to earn any of it?

Sitting on the bed again, Rincon tugged on his boots. He was deep in dark thought when Elizabeth returned with a quart of whiskey wrapped in a brown paper sack.

She slapped the bottle down on the table, sighed with exasperation and sagged onto the bed.

'Now what's the matter with you?' Rincon asked, as he walked to the table, uncorked the bottle and poured himself three fingers of raw spirit.

'Nothing!' Elizabeth said with sarcasm. 'What could be wrong? I am sitting in a dirty hotel room we can't even afford to pay for, watching you drink cheap whiskey while your partner is laid up in bed with a gunshot wound. And you haven't even got a plan to get us out of this.'

'I didn't say I hadn't a plan,' Rincon said, walking to the window. He parted the curtains and stood looking down at the street, glass in hand.

'Then tell me . . . what, Rincon!' Elizabeth said with exasperation. He did not answer. His eyes remained fixed on the street below. The wild card had just been played.

He watched as the three weary men on tired horses, bearded and trail-dusty, rode up the street through the new morning light, and cursed.

'What is it?' Elizabeth asked, coming to join him at the window.

'The Whittaker brothers,' Rincon said, before taking another sip of whiskey.

'Are you sure?' Elizabeth asked, drawing back a corner of the curtains to peer out at the arriving riders. 'You said you've never seen them.'

'I've seen their brother – dead and alive – they're all out of the same mold. I don't like this, Elizabeth, I don't like it a bit.'

Because the plan Rincon had been formulating had just flown out the window. With Cal Mercer down, it had seemed the right time to go after this Ben Flowers once again, remove him and search the ranch inch by inch. Now the Whittakers were back, and they knew about Mercer. They knew about Rincon, and they would quite cheerfully gun either of them down on sight.

SIX

Ned Whittaker was suffering though a gloomy drunk that morning. Carl and Barstow were no help. Ned wished that their youngest brother, Walt were still alive. Or Deuce. Or Jacob. They were the more reliable of all of the brothers. Deuce and Jacob had stayed on managing the old ranch while the rest of them wandered the plains looking for a quick score. Their last effort had gotten young Walt shot down outside a Bismarck bank and the rest of them had fled empty-handed. It was a tough life, and they had little to show for trying to run shortcuts.

Ned was thinking that it was time to quit riding the outlaw trail. Carl and Barstow might be convinced that their time had passed. Ned had talked them into the wild living, he should be able to talk them out of it.

Nearing fifty, his beard now more gray than black, Ned had just about had enough.

He knew about the shootout on the old ranch, not all of it, but enough to know that Deuce and Jacob had been gunned down. The talk was that the army had done it – why they were involved was not clear to Ned who had been in Colorado at the time. But it was said also that the man who had done the actual shooting was an old prairie wolf named Calvin Mercer and his partner, a Texas gunnie named Rincon. Why this had come about, Ned did not know and never would learn now that both Deuce and Jacob were dead, but one day his path would cross that of those who had done the killing, and the reasons would not matter. The Whittaker family took care of itself, and blood would pay for blood.

'What are you doing, Ned?' Barstow Whittaker asked, rising from the bed he had been sharing with his brother, Carl. He rubbed his shaggy head and walked to the table where their morning whiskey sat.

'Thinking about staying home,' Ned Whittaker answered. 'Maybe Deuce and Jacob had the right idea all along. Clean up the old ranch and stick to the place. I, myself, am tired of running from the law, sleeping on rocky ground and eating whatever we happen to run across.'

'You're serious, aren't you?' Barstow responded, sagging into a chair to drink whiskey from the bottle. 'You mean you're ready to go straight?'

'What's all of our rambling gotten us, Barstow?' Ned responded in a booming voice. 'I don't know – maybe it was seeing Walt get shot to pieces in that Bismarck job . . . something. But I'm suddenly tired, Brother.'

'Maybe you just need some time to rest up,' Barstow answered, again tilting the bottle.

'Maybe,' Ned said wearily. 'Maybe that's it. Either way I mean to go back to the ranch for awhile. Like we used to do.'

'Didn't you hear?' Barstow asked, corking the bottle. 'That fellow told us last night that some nester had taken the place over.'

'I heard,' Ned growled. 'You tell me if that sounds right. Some people, the army maybe, come in and shoot down Deuce and Jacob so that they're too dead to pay their taxes and someone else who never worked a day building the property up can just lay claim to it!' Ned Whittaker's voice kept rising in volume, so that Carl Whittaker, too, stirred in his bed. 'You tell me that's right, Barstow!'

'I didn't say it was right,' Barstow said cautiously. His older brother was unpredictable when riled. 'I said it was the law.'

'The law,' Ned Whittaker scoffed. 'It's a little late in the day for us to be worrying about what the law says.' He walked to the table, uncorked and tilted the bottle himself. Cuffing off his mouth, he told his brother, 'That ranch is ours. We're taking it back.'

'Need any more?' Kate McCallister asked, standing near the stack of shingles as Ben Flowers's hammer rang on the roof above.

'No, I think that's got it!' he shouted down. 'I guess I won't know until it rains again. Looking skyward, he commented, 'Which might not be too long from now, judging from those thunderheads.'

'Well, climb on down and call it day,' Kate suggested. 'As you say, you won't know until it happens, but no matter, you have made an improvement.'

'I suppose you're right,' Ben answered. 'Stand back. I'm going to toss some of these old shingles down.'

'I'm clear!' Kate called up.

The rotten, weathered old shingles began to fall from the roof, and then Ben climbed onto the top of the ladder, and Elizabeth steadied it as the tired-appearing young man came down, bucket of nails still strapped to his belt, hammer thrust behind his waistband.

Standing on firm ground once again he grinned at her, wiped back his dark curly hair and said, 'That was a day – I don't like that sort of work.'

'Ben . . . you're not still mad at me, are you?'

'Was I mad at you?' he asked, putting his hands on her slender waist. 'If I was, I didn't mean it. It's just that these are rough times for me. And,' he added, 'I don't know if I could have made it this far if not for you. So, no, I am not mad at you.'

More quietly he said, 'But you might tell your father that we have no understanding between us. I barely know you, girl.'

'I'll tell him,' Kate said in a chilly voice. Abruptly she turned away. 'I have to see to Buck.'

Ben watched her walk away toward the lean-to where the ponies were sheltered. He felt that again he had said the wrong thing at the wrong time. What was a man to do? They had no understanding between them, and he wasn't going to be railroaded into a situation he was unready for. If she could not understand that, well. . . .

Kate had saddled her buckskin horse and now rode away from him, her slender figure erect in the saddle, her eyes fixed on the trail ahead. Again she did not wave or call back. Again he felt her absence almost immediately, and he knew that the cabin, whether it rained or not, would once again be cold and empty. Angrily he shuffled off with his tools toward the storage shed.

Well, what did she expect? He restrained the sudden impulse to hurl his hammer and trudged on.

Any reasonable woman, he thought, as he put his tools and hardware away, would understand that a man alone might wish for a woman, but if he was not in a position to support her, the timing was wrong. A reasonable woman would understand that they did not know each other very well at all, and that these things took time.

Why was she so unreasonable?

And why did he wish that he was less cautious?

Because the presence of that skinny little girl with the sawed off black hair made his days brighter, her absence made his nights lonelier, being with her made his efforts all seem worthwhile.

Rincon was saddling his tall black horse with the white stockings. Nightfall was not far distant, and he had observed the Whittaker brothers, looking drunk as skunks, trailing out of town. He intended to follow them. From their demeanor, he sensed that they were intent on dangerous business. That, he considered, could only mean that they were going to pay a visit to their brothers' former ranch.

Had they yet learned about the gold? There was no way of knowing, but it was a risk Rincon could not take. He had not spent five years in prison, dreaming about how he would spend the money, only to lose it to these rough-shod border bandits.

Cal Mercer was still laid up in bed, angry and touchy as a sick child. Now, to top it all, Calvin had begun drinking again himself, believing it was the best way to kill the pain in his leg. Calvin Mercer was a mean man sober. Even Rincon did not relish being around a drunken Mercer.

They had ridden too many trails together.

Well, he thought as he swung into leather, his business with Cal was over now that he had gotten himself shot up. If Elizabeth was right about nothing else, she was correct in that: they either had to get away from Cal or . . . get rid of him. Rincon started his leggy black up the dusk-shrouded street as lanterns flickered on across the tiny Great Plains town.

Ben Flowers looked to the western sky which was the color of lilac with crimson streaks sketched jaggedly across it. He stood, coffee cup in hand on the porch of the cabin, feeling quite pleased with himself about the way the work was shaping up, quite disappointed with himself for the manner in which he seemed to be mishandling affairs with Kate McCallister. He cared about the girl, truly did, but a sort of tension had crept into their relationship that he did not know how to resolve.

The sky darkened. Ben went into the cabin,

poked at the low-burning fire, sagged into a chair and stared ahead. Everything was going as well as could be expected . . . and yet. He let his chin lower toward his chest and allowed his eyelids to drop as the warm glow of the fire soothed him.

How long he dozed, he could not have said, but the fire was burned down to softly glowing embers when the crash at the door awakened him.

Again!

He leapt from the chair, half-rolled toward the door, grabbing for his Colt as the first shots thudded into the new oaken planks. He counted six in all. Only two slugs penetrated the green wood. Seated braced against the opposite wall, Ben began methodically emptying his pistol into the door.

Outside a man howled, a man cursed. Three more shots penetrated the door. Ben sank to his belly and fired upward at the intruders. Distantly then he heard the sound of a rifle crackling. There was a brief, excited exchange between the men on the porch and then they bounded for their horses.

Not eager to run into their guns, Ben waited

a minute before he eased out onto the porch. He could hear ponies galloping away and then a horse approaching the cabin. Hugh hailed the house before emerging from the shadows.

'They just won't give up, will they?' McCallister's ranch hand said, halting his roan horse in front of the cabin, tilting back his hat.

'No,' Ben said, grimly reloading his revolver. 'They just won't give up.' Looking around, he holstered his pistol and told Hugh, 'I do appreciate you backing me up. Without your rifle, I think they would have breached the door.'

'Ben,' Hugh said, 'I wasn't the one shooting at them. Nor was it Dusty. I don't know who the hell it was.'

'You caught not a glimpse of them? Any of them?'

'Not a glimpse.' Hugh was silent for a time as his horse blew and stamped impatiently. 'What do you plan to do now, Ben?'

'I can't live forted up like this. I can't let some rifleman pick me off as I go about my daily chores,' Ben Flowers said deliberately. 'I mean to do what must be done – I'm going to track them down and take the battle to them.'

*

Rincon sat his black horse on the low knoll, deliberately reloading his Winchester. He could have taken all three of the Whittaker brothers out but he had sensed, then caught a glimpse of the other riders in the night. Who they were, where they had come from he did not know. This was all getting too complicated. What had seemed a simple plan in its conception had become a tangle.

No one was supposed to be on the ranch. Now he had the nester, this Ben Flowers, the three Whittaker brothers and two other men he could not identify who seemed to be working for or with Flowers.

On top of that Calvin Mercer was laid up, probably drunk and useless for anything but making a bad situation worse as he had already proven. Rincon rubbed his forehead with the heel of his hand, for the moment wishing he was anywhere but here.

But *here* was where the gold was. Wasn't it?

He wondered briefly if the nester had already found where Billy Carter had stashed the army gold, maybe hired two men to help him protect it. There was no way of knowing for certain. Rincon had the momentary urge just to ride away from the confusion, but where would that leave him? No, he had five years invested in this already. He would end up dragging the line, looking for hand-outs. Elizabeth, such as she was, would certainly strike out on her own as well.

He needed that twenty thousand. Fully intended to have it.

It was small consolation that he had tagged one of the Whittaker boys with a well-aimed shot, but anything that cut the odds down a little was a step ahead. Grimly Rincon turned his black horse back toward Pawnee Town.

Thunder growled and bone-white lightning was streaking the long skies over the Dakota plains by the time Ben Flowers had saddled his sorrel and started down the long trail toward Pawnee. Hugh had nearly convinced him that it was a fool's errand, but he was good and mad now. He was just trying to make an honest living, to build a small place of his own, and they kept coming! Men he did not know, had no grudge against and should have had none against him, threatening to destroy the little he had managed to build up. For himself and for. . . .

For himself.

The cold wind frolicked and then roared across the plains. Still dim moonlight shone through the gathered clouds, and Ben was able to pick out the tracks of three horses bee-lining it toward Pawnee. One of these was ill-shod, another had a chip in its right fore horseshoe. He thought he would be able to identify these again should he manage to catch up.

They were certainly riding toward the town. There was no other place to shelter up on the vast plains. And, at least one of them was wounded. Badly wounded. He knew this because following them, he had come upon a sandy patch of earth near a creek crossing where a man had fallen from his horse. The sign was all too obvious even in the near-darkness of the arriving storm.

Either Ben had tagged one of them through the door or the mysterious rifleman – and who could that be? – had done some damage. There were too many pieces to the puzzle. It should have been quite simple, but men kept popping up, firing their weapons and disappearing in ways that he could not fit together. It seemed the world was against him. 'Well,' he muttered, 'look out world, here I come.'

He was no soldier, no gunhand, no hero, but he had been pushed to his limit, and a man would do wild things when he reached that limit.

'What happened?' Elizabeth Cole asked, when Rincon stamped into the room, his shoulders damp with the first raindrops of the gathering storm. He grunted something that was no answer, propped his rifle up in the corner and flung his hat aside, seating himself on the bed.

'I don't know,' he said eventually, rubbing vigorously at his head. 'I followed the Whittaker boys to the ranch. They stormed it. Someone shot back from inside. I jumped in, took a shot at the Whittakers. Then two other riders – I don't know who they were – showed up and I decided it was time to cut out.'

'Meaning we're no closer to the gold than we were a couple of days ago,' Elizabeth said. There was a chill to her voice. The rain began to splat heavily against the window of their hotel room. Again Rincon declined to answer her. 'We can't even afford to spend another night here,' she said, 'unless you have some hide-out cash.'

'I don't,' Rincon said flatly. 'I'll talk to the

manager in the morning. Maybe we could sell your horse,' he suggested.

'Fine. And leave me afoot in a strange town. We could sell *your* horse, Rincon!' She sagged onto the bed, 'But where would that leave us? Both of us. I should have known better.'

'The gold is there. It's mine. I'm going to get it!' he said in a furious voice. Elizabeth had placed her hand on his shoulder; now he brushed it aside and stood to go to the window to watch the driving rain, silver in the scattered lamplights as it fell from the black, rumbling skies. 'I will have it,' he said in a voice cold enough to chill the room. Elizabeth shuddered at his tone, folded her hands together between her knees, watched Rincon.

And she wondered.

'It all has to be done before Cal is up on his feet again, doesn't it?' she said carefully.

'It's best,' Rincon said, not turning his eyes back to the room. 'I've got to eliminate the Whittaker boys first.'

'There's three of them!' Elizabeth said. She sounded more excited than concerned.

'I think only two now. The advantage is that I know who they are; they can't know me on sight.'

'It's dangerous work, Rincon,' Elizabeth said.

'Isn't it?' he said tightly. 'But there's no other way. I'm going to go hunting them. Then – if I don't come back, you can sell my horse, catch the next stage and be damned!'

Elizabeth bowed her head and cried, but she was not fooling Rincon – nor herself.

SEVEN

Carl Whittaker was not going to make it. That much was obvious as Ned and Barstow removed his trousers and surveyed the damage the rifle slug had done to his leg. Barstow sat back on his heels and tipped his hat from his brow.

'What are we going to do, Ned? What can we do now? There's only the two of us left.'

'I don't know. I have to think about it,' Ned said, sagging into the only chair in the ratty room. He picked up the whiskey bottle, found it empty and flung it away to break against the wall.

'We don't even know who shot him,' Barstow muttered.

'No, but we know who was responsible. The nester. I will get him, Barstow, watch and see. If we never get our ranch hack, I will get him.'

Barstow watched Carl Whittaker dying on the bed. Carl's leg twitched, his mouth opened and he groaned out muffled words of pain and despair.

'I can't take this any more,' Barstow said, rising. 'I'm going out to find a bottle of whiskey. You coming?'

'No,' Ned replied heavily. 'One of us ought to be here when Carl passes. Ask around and find out if they've got an undertaker in this town, will you, Barstow? Tell him we likely have some work for him to do and,' he added grimly, 'tell him I'll be sending some more trade his way real soon.'

Barstow nodded and stepped outside of the ramshackle rooming-house. The rain had begun to drive down with intensity. Hunching his shoulders, he stepped off into the alleyway and made his way toward the saloon opposite.

Ben Flowers rode his rain-glossed sorrel pony up the muddy street into Pawnee. The wind was chill on his back. Distantly thunder rumbled. The storm was not gong to abate any time soon. Lanterns shone dully behind windows where the townspeople sheltered in their homes. No one was abroad except for one wide-shouldered, bearded man slogging his way toward the saloon. Ben continued on toward the stables. He thought he could identify the horses the attackers had ridden. They would be wet and hard-ridden, one with a misaligned shoe, the other wearing a shoe with a chip in it on the right front hoof. How many men could have been out riding hard on this night with those distinctive flaws on their horseshoes? Few, and the stable hand would be able to identify them for him.

Ben did not wish to fight, certainly did not wish to kill anybody, but damnit, they would not leave him alone! How could he ever have any peace of mind as he tried to go about his work, constantly worrying about snipers or bold raiders?

He swung down from the sorrel and led it into the musty confines of the stable. A lantern hung on a nail near the entrance, but no one seemed to be there. Ben took a few minutes to wipe down his cold, shuddering horse with a burlap sack, looped its reins loosely around a stall rail and went searching for the stable hand.

There must be someone around. Men came and went at all hours in such a place of business, and no one would wander off leaving a lantern burning in a building filled with dry hay.

He walked from one end of the stable to the other, calling out, but there was no answer. Halfway down he found three horses – a gray, a roan and a stubby little dun, their heads hanging with fatigue. They had not been here long – he could still see the dampness of their coats, the dry patches where their saddles had rested.

He eased into their stalls one by one. It took sometime, but he found the shoe which was missing two nails and had gone slightly askew on the roan. The little dun had a large chip in the horseshoe on its right front hoof.

'Hey, what are you doing back there!'

A small man, nearly bald, his gray whiskers unshorn, approached Ben, holding a lantern high. His mouth was tight with suspicion. Ben adopted a smile.

'Wondered where you were! I was checking out these three ponies. They belong to some friends of mine. We lost sight of each other on the trail when the storm settled in.'

'Did you?' the little man said dubiously. He

had had too many horses stolen from under his nose to trust any stranger.

'They can't have arrived more than an hour ago,' Ben said, slipping out of the stall, still carrying his smile. 'Did you see them?'

The stable hand still hesitated, his eyes wary behind the light cast by his lantern.

Ben used the oldest friend-making inducement in the world. He dipped a handful of silver dollars from his rocket and said, 'I'll need to stable up my sorrel here for awhile, too. We're all beat. It was a long trail.'

Silver can make a man's caution break down. The stable hand lowered his lantern and turned his attention to the sorrel, stroking its neck. 'You got away clean, did you?' he asked.

'What's that?' Ben asked.

'Your friends. They said they were hit by a band of Cheyenne Indians. One of them got himself shot up pretty good.'

'You don't mean it!' Ben said, continuing the charade. 'It must have happened after we split up. I have to find them now. Any idea where they could be?'

'There's only two places for passers-by to lay up in Pawnee,' the stableman said, uncinching the sorrel's saddle. 'The hotel and the . . . well, they call it a boarding-house, I'd call it a flop-house, over on Third Street. Were you gents carrying much money?'

'No. I was the banker, and you saw what I have. Maybe ten dollars at the most.'

'Then they'll be in the flophouse on Third.' The stable hand slipped the saddle from the sorrel's back and with more strength than a man his size would seem to possess, he flipped it up and positioned it easily over a rail. 'Unless you want to carry it with you,' he said, knowing that some men would rather lose anything before their saddles.

'Not tonight. I'll trust you with it. Third Street you say . . . are you sure they're the men I'm talking about? What did they look like?'

'All big, husky with black beards,' the stable hand said. Now the wariness had returned to his eyes.

'That's them all right,' Ben said. *Who were they?* 'Give the sorrel a scoop of oats, will you? He's earned it.' Then he went out before the small man could ask him any questions. Glancing back as he went into the rain, Ben saw the stable hand standing in the shelter of the doorway, watching after him curiously.

Rain sheeted down. The faces of the buildings were screened with coldly dripping water. There was a covered plankwalk in front of only a few of the structures. One of them was a hotel with an adjoining restaurant. It took him a few minutes to find Third Street. There was a white wooden sign with crude lettering nailed to a post and an arrow pointing in the direction of 'Nell's Boarding-house'.

He started that way through the rain, his heart feeling tight inside his chest.

The boarding-house was a low sprawling collection of four different cabins, nearly abutting. There was a light burning in only one of these and Ben started that way. He was not at all sure that he was up to this, but there was no other way to stop the raiding. Through the rain he walked toward the door of the lighted cabin, his boots sliding in the thick red mud underfoot.

The small porch was covered only at the doorway. Ben stepped up to knock, but the door stood ajar. Someone else, it seemed was expected. Drawing his Colt, Ben Flowers slipped into the room. There were two men there. One dozing in a chair, arms crossed, a second dying on the nearby cot.

'Whittaker?' Ben said, and the man in the chair opened his heavy eyelids.

'Who the hell are you?' Ned Whittaker asked in a dull voice. Ben noticed the empty whiskey bottle which had broken against the wall. Beyond the single small window, lightning flashed again.

'My name's Ben Flowers,' he replied, and sudden fury filled the big bearded man's eyes.

'You! You're the one who shot my brother down.' His eyes rolled toward the cot where the man with the waxen face groaned in soft surrender.

'I shot nobody down,' Ben said, moving further into the room. 'But you have been trying to kill me. Why, I'm not sure, but I've come to put a halt to it.' Ben watched Ned Whittaker's eyes roam the room, going from the fireplace to the corner where his rifle leaned against the shabby wall, to the Colt revolver which rested in its holster on a gunbelt hanging over the hack of the chair, to the front door as if he expected help. Maybe he did.

Ben eased that way and shut the door, pulling

in the drawstring. The barely living flesh on the cot moaned again; and there was a gurgling sound deep in his throat.

'You've killed my brother,' Ned said. He started to rise from the chair, but Ben cautioned him with the muzzle of his Colt. 'You or one of your crew.'

'I have no crew,' Ben said firmly. 'You're not going to tell me why you tried to shoot me down?'

'Why!' Ned laughed and growled at the same time. 'You dumb nester. Because it's our ranch you're living on, always has been.'

'No. It belonged to your two brothers. They're both dead. None of the rest of you cared enough to come back and stay on the land or even to pay the taxes.'

'We have been pursuing other interests,' Ned said coldly. His eyes again searched the room from point to point.

'For five years?' Ned asked.

'That doesn't matter, does it? We're back now. We've come to claim what is ours.'

'But it's not yours, Whittaker. And it never was!' Ben Flowers forced himself to stay calm. 'I bought the place, legally. I am out there working on the ranch every day. It is my land now, and there I'll stay.'

'Until the day you die,' Ned said with quiet menace.

'Until then, yes.' The two men stared at each other. Firelight flickered and cast wavering shadows across their determined faces. Neither spoke for a long minute.

The silence was broken by yet another peal of close thunder. Ben kept his Colt level and cocked. There was no mistaking the murderous intent in Ned Whittaker's eyes. Even a moment's inattention could prompt the bearded man to make his move.

'You're with them, aren't you?' Ned asked at length, lowering his arms. His hands clenched the arms of the wooden chair tightly.

'I haven't any idea what you're talking about.'

'Them that got my brothers out on the ranch.'

'I've heard that the army killed them,' Ben replied. He was inclined to let Ned talk – there were still puzzling elements to all this. Was there more behind this than the Whittaker brothers wanting their hide-out back?

'I've heard the story told that way, too,' Ned

said, shifting in his chair in a way Ben didn't care for, as if he were positioning his legs. 'But you tell me, nester, why would the army ride all the way down here to start a fighting war with Deuce and Jacob? Does that make sense to you?'

Ben was silent, pondering Ned's words. No – it didn't really make a lot of sense. But then he had no idea of what the other Whittaker brothers had been up to.

'Who then?' Ben asked quietly. A log in the fireplace popped as flames hit pitch.

'It was that plains wolf, Mercer, and that Texas gunhand, Rincon.'

'Never heard of them,' Ben said honestly.

'So you say,' Ned Whittaker.

'Why did they do it then?'

'Those two? They'd shoot a man down for his boots.' Ned stretched his arms and then suddenly yelled toward the cot where the dying man lay. 'Get him, Carl!'

Ben Flowers glanced that way and Ned Whittaker launched himself from the chair.

The big man plowed into Ben. His shoulder caught Ben under his arm and his hand jerked up, and the Colt flew free. Ned kept his feet driving and carried Ben across the tiny room to slam him against the wall. The breath rushed from Ben Flowers. Before he could recover, the bearded man winged two chopping blows into his ribs then tried for Ben's jaw. Ben managed to duck under the overhand right and scuttle away on the floor, trying to reach his pistol. Ned kicked him in passing, his boot toe driving into Ben's ribs. Ben felt something crack, and jagged pain flooded his torso.

He scrambled toward his Colt, but Ned Whittaker managed to snatch at and grab his belt. He dragged Ben back and started for the gun himself, but Ben managed to kick out and catch the big man on the kneecap. Ned went down howling with pain.

Lightning flared against the window pane. Silver rain slanted down torrentially. Half-bent over, Ben stood trying to catch his breath, watching as Ned Whittaker turned cautiously toward him and then lunged toward his rifle. Ben hurled himself at the bearded man's knees and brought him down to the floor. Ned's chin hit the planks hard as he was tackled and he seemed momentarily dazed.

Staggering away, Ben again reached for his pistol, but before he had picked it up, Ned

Whittaker was on him again with a roar of fury. They fell against the wooden chair, breaking it. Ben saw Ned's own Colt which had been hanging there by his gunbelt and grabbed at it desperately.

His head was knocked against the rail of the cot as they fell to the ground and he was briefly stunned. He was now on his back on the floor, Ned Whittaker straddling him, winging wild rights and lefts to Ben's head.

A cold hand dropped from the edge of the cot and landed across Ben Flowers's face. Enraged, Ned renewed his attack, striking his dead brother's arm as often as he struck Ben. Ben could not fight back, pinned as he was, but his clawing fingers found something cool, smooth and familiar. Frantically he twisted and writhed, trying to grasp the Colt revolver. Ned continued to drive down powerful blows which Ben could no longer roll away from. Dizzy now, beaten and breathing raggedly, he knew it was only a matter of time before he was battered to death. His scrabbling fingers reached the butt of the pistol. curled around it. His thumb drew back the hammer and twisting his hand into an awkward position he fired off as thunder roared outside.

And shot Ned Whittaker in the back.

The .44 slug entered at the small of Ned's back, and firing up as Ben was, it angled upward and caught the bearded man's heart. The bullet did not exit. Ned's mouth filled with blood and he made a gurgling sound much as his brother had. His fist still uplifted to strike again, he died and rolled from on top of Ben to lie motionless on the cold floor.

Ben Flowers lay still for a long minute as gunsmoke curled across the room to join the smoke the green wood in the fireplace was spewing up the chimney.

Finally, effortfully, he rolled Ned's body from him and rose to his feet, using the cot as support. For a long while he stood there, bent over the corpse of Carl Whittaker, unable to straighten up. His ribs were battered, his head hummed with confusion.

He brought himself erect, stretched out a hand to pull the blanket over Carl Whittaker's face and stumbled across the room. Recovering his own Colt he threw Ned's aside. If anyone had heard the gunshot, no one was in a hurry to rush out into the storm to investigate. Ben wanted to rest, to bathe his battered face, to lie down and sleep.

Instead he staggered toward the door to the room, flung it open to the night and stepped out into the rage of the storm. Ben only wanted to reach the stable, to find his sorrel and somehow make it back to his ranch. It was too late.

Before he had stepped off the porch, Barstow Whittaker appeared at the head of the alley.

EIGHT

Barstow Whittaker had stopped for a few drinks in the saloon before he purchased a bottle to take back to the boarding-house. He had asked about an undertaker, but the town had none. That meant that there would be some digging for them to do whenever the rain stopped. Ned would likely be angry that it had taken him so long, but that couldn't be helped. Barstow had not liked sitting in the small room watching Carl die slowly. A little air had been called for, a little whiskey even if it required a long walk in the rain.

Ducking his head into the constant downpour, Barstow trooped toward the little shack where his brothers waited. A shaft of light fell across the rain-pocked alleyway and Barstow halted, frowning It was unlikely that Ned would be coming out into the rain. Peering through the steel mesh of rain, Barstow saw the figure silhouetted in the firelit doorway. It was not Ned. This man was much thinner, a little taller. Who. . . ? Barstow hastened on.

When he was within a dozen paces of the open door, Barstow could see past the stranger, see that Ned lay sprawled on the floor, his eyes open, seeing nothing. Barstow shouted out, 'Hey, you!'

Whoever it was spun toward him, Colt in his hand. Barstow dropped the bottle of whiskey he had been carrying and pawed at his holstered revolver. Standing in the screen of rain, Barstow deliberately raised his weapon and took aim. Both men touched off at once. Either through skill or blind chance, the man on the porch tagged Barstow with his first shot, while Barstow's slug flew completely through the cabin, shattering the far window.

Barstow cursed, swatted at his wounded arm, and started away at a staggering run.

Ben Flowers had no doubt who the bearded man was. He lurched toward the edge of the porch and stepped down. Holding his ribs with one hand, he ran – if that word described his stumbling, careering motion – after Barstow Whittaker.

The rain was heavy enough to be blinding, stinging his eyes. As he ran on, taking in sharp short breaths, Ben considered – where would Barstow run to? It had to be toward the stable to catch up his pony to try to escape on the great plains. Ben staggered on, his pace no more rapid than the wounded Barstow's. As he left the alleyway, the unbroken wind became a thrusting force against his rain-soaked body. He could not see Barstow. The rain continued; dark clouds seemed nearly to touch the earth. Even the lights in the windows of the various buildings were mostly obscured in the night storm.

He found the stable more by memory than sight and eased up beside the open double doors. Inside the lantern still burned. There was no sign of Barstow Whittaker. Perhaps, Ben thought, he had made a mistake. But then a horse whickered uneasily, and Ben just made out a low groan of human complaint.

Grimly he entered the high-roofed barn, his Colt's barrel held high beside his ear. Halfway along the row of stalls, a man was struggling mightily with a saddle. It was Barstow. Ben cried out one warning, 'Stand where you are!' and instantly wished that he hadn't for Barstow spun clumsily, went to one knee and fired twice, the bullets spinning off into the wall behind Ben. The horses almost in unison reared up or kicked at their stalls in a panicked urge to run away from trouble.

Ben threw himself to one side, sending a spasm of fiery pain through his damaged chest. Barstow fired again, then again, his bullets gouging splinters from the boards of the stall where Ben had taken shelter.

The stable fell silent. Peering up over the stall, Ben found that he could no longer see Barstow. Ben's hair was in his eyes, his clothing coldly plastered to his body, his ribs fiery with pain. How long could this go on? Even as that thought passed through his mind, Barstow Whittaker popped up from behind a nearer stall and fired again, his face brutally angry, his black eyes wild.

Ben was not quicker this time, but his shot was truer. A .44 slug from his Colt revolver punched through the half-inch thick planks of the stall and tagged Barstow, sending him staggering back across the compartment under the neck of a frightened piebald horse. Ben waited. There was no more movement in the stable.

Thumbing back the hammer of his Colt he eased out of the stall and carefully approached the spot where Barstow Whittaker had vanished. Wide horse eyes followed his passage. Gunsmoke still hung heavily in the air.

Barstow lay dead on his back, his gun flung to one side, his eyes open and somehow venomous even in death. Ben holstered his revolver and leaned back against a wooden post, doubled over with pain.

A lantern, a moving shadow caught his eye and he stiffened. It was the old stableman approaching, lamp in one hand, shotgun in the other. Reaching the scene, he eyed the battered Ben Flowers and then the dead Barstow Whittaker.

'Well,' he said dryly, 'I see that you found your friends.'

The sorrel was in no mood to leave the warmth of the stable and go out again into the cold, stormy night, but Ben was in no mood to remain in Pawnee and answer questions. What he wanted was his own warmth, his own home, his own fire burning and so he pushed the sorrel onward through the stormy night. Somewhere ahead lay safety and security, a small measure of comfort.

It was over – the men who had come to steal his land, using murder if necessary, were dead, every one of them. That was enough to bring a cold, guilty feeling into Ben's stomach, but what other choice had there been? The fiery pain in his ribs drove all moral considerations from his mind. They would have had no compunction at all about shooting him down, he knew. Bowing his head to the rain, he pressed the sorrel on toward the home ranch.

'I didn't think I'd make it,' Ben Flowers said from the cot where he lay.

'You didn't. Dusty and Hugh found you about a quarter-mile out, lying in the mud.'

'They brought me home?'

'We did,' Kate McCallister said. 'What kind of fool's errand were you on anyway?'

'I needed to protect my home,' Ben said weakly. He started to tell her what had happened, but Kate gestured for him to be silent. There was a fire burning in the hearth, and some sort of soup or broth boiling. He touched his ribs gingerly. They had been bound very tightly by someone – Kate, he assumed. Now she drew his blankets up and sat beside him in one of the wooden chairs. Dressed in her good white dress with the blue ribbons, she looked angelic to his fevered eyes.

'How long was I out?' he asked.

'Nearly twenty-four hours,' Kate told him.

'Can't have been!' he objected.

'You were,' she assured him. 'And you talk in your sleep, Ben.'

'Nothing foolish, I hope,' he said, looking up at the skinny little dark-haired girl.

'Mostly foolish,' she answered, and she seemed to blush faintly. She took his hand in both of hers and said gently, 'Rest now – or if you'd like there's some barley soup you can try first.'

'Soup sounds good,' he said around a yawn. 'My horse!'

'He's OK. He has more sense than you. He made it home. That's how we knew to go out and look for you on the back trail.'

'How did anybody . . . were you waiting here

for me all that time, Kate?'

'What do you think?' she asked, rising. 'I'll fetch the soup.'

He was asleep again before she returned, but this time his dreams were more tranquil and pain and fears did not reach him.

'The storm's finally broken,' Rincon said, as he turned from the window. His once-handsome face was growing haggard. He never smiled. They were now three days behind on paying for their hotel room. The manager had told Elizabeth Cole that he would have thrown them out except for the storm into which he wouldn't send anybody.

'I still can't believe that Flowers got the Whittaker brothers,' Elizabeth said. She herself was looking tired, she decided, as she brushed her blonde hair in front of the oval mirror.

'He did! They found the bodies. When I went over to beg the stable hand to shelter our horses for one more day, he told me that he saw a part of it. You and your "greener"!'

'Ben Flowers never struck me as being very dangerous,' Elizabeth told Rincon who remained scowling out at the gradually clearing skies, the wind-shifted clouds.

'Looks can be deceiving,' Rincon growled. 'Anyway, he's cleared out all the underbrush.'

'I don't understand you,' Elizabeth said, turning from the mirror.

'I mean I don't have to worry about the Whittaker brothers anymore. There's just me and the nester.'

'You're still going to try it?' she asked.

'Of course. What else is there to do? Stick up a bank? There's still twenty-thousand gold dollars on that ranch, Elizabeth. Twenty-thousand of *my* gold dollars.'

'How do you mean to do it?' she asked with nervous anticipation.

'I don't know yet. Not for sure. But Ben Flowers doesn't know me. I can get close enough to him to figure a way, to find the right moment. And I will, Elizabeth. I promise you that I will.'

Again visions of a life filled with silk and satin and warm comfort crowded together in the back of Elizabeth Cole's mind and she went to Rincon, tenderly putting her arms around the gunman's waist resting her cheek against his chest.

*

When Ben Flowers next awakened, the door to the cabin stood open. The day outside was bright. The smell of paint pervaded the air. He sat up in bed, wiping the sleep from his eyes.

'What's going on around here!' he called out.

'Oh good, you're awake,' Kate McCallister said cheerfully. She appeared in the doorway in black jeans, red-checked shirt, a bandanna tied over her head. She was holding a paint brush. 'I'm just about finished with the front room. I wanted to do that area next.'

'Save it for another day,' Ben grumbled, lying back. 'I don't feel too good.'

'No more nursing,' Kate said. 'Time for you to get up, feed yourself and get some work done.'

'I'm just not up to it, Kate,' Ben complained.

'Sure you are. I'm not telling you to dig a ditch, just get up and move about a little. I'm warning you,' she said, shaking her paintbrush. 'I'm going to come in there and start on the walls in about fifteen minutes. You won't like it much if you're not up and out of there.'

'Who are you bossing around?' Ben growled.

'Is this your house or mine?'

'It's yours,' Kate answered, 'and I think it's high time you got back to trying to fix it up.'

'You're a cruel woman,' Ben muttered, swinging his feet to the floor. Kate laughed and returned to her work.

She was right, of course, but he still didn't feel up to attempting much. His cracked ribs were shot through with pain. There was a lump on his head and his teeth ached. Nevertheless, he rose, reached for his hat and his jeans, tugged his boots on – with much effort – and rose from the cot. His back hurt as well on this morning. He looked at the sagging cot with its inch-thick mattress.

'I've got to find a way to get a real bed.' He spoke a little louder. 'Does anyone sell beds in Pawnee?'

'They can order you one out of Fargo. Probably take a week.'

Ben stood in the connecting doorway, watching the energetic woman paint. She was standing on a plank laid over two sawhorses, finishing up the section of wall near the ceiling. He was still shirtless; he scratched at the bandages binding his chest.

'Aren't you going to finish dressing?' Kate asked, glancing at him.

'I don't think I can maneuver my way into a shirt.'

'Oh, for. . . !' Kate stepped down from the sawhorse platform, brushed past him and went into the tiny sleeping area. She took a shirt from his kit, shook it out and returned. 'I'm starting to lose patience with you, Ben. Lift up this arm.'

Ben complied. He didn't like being bossed around, but in some distant way it was pleasant to be fussed over.

'Any of that barley soup left?' he asked.

'Most of it. It's not hot, though.'

'I don't care. It's food,' he answered.

'There's also some bread I brought over from home,' she called, as she got back to work.

Ben nodded without replying, walked unsteadily to the pantry and began digging out the few bits of kitchenware he had. A bowl, a spoon, a bread knife. It wasn't much of a breakfast, but it settled well and by the time he was through he felt better for having been forced from his bed. The general tightness in his battered body was subsiding as he moved around although his ribs continued to complain with each too-sudden movement he made.

'I'm going out to see to my horse,' he called to Kate, who had moved her materials into the sleeping area.

'He's all right,' she answered.

'I said I'm going out to see to my sorrel,' he repeated. 'What am I, an invalid?'

He thought he heard a little chirp of laughter in response. Going to the open door he paused to look around. The cabin looked nothing like the dump he had first entered. He had done the flooring, but the rest of it was Kate's work. Fresh white paint, the kitchen orderly. Now he noticed for the first time that there was an oval-shaped braided rug in tan and deep maroon near the fireplace. He frowned, shook his head and went out into the bright morning.

Ben stretched his arms, was immediately sorry that he had as pain flashed across his chest, and walked toward the lean-to where the two horses stood side by side – the sorrel and Kate's shaggy buckskin. A group of crows, unhappy with his approach, rose from the branches of the oak tree, flew in a lazy circle and landed again, chasing him with a chorus of raucous cawing. Maybe they had thought they had won a victory

Ben stroked the sorrel's neck. The horse glanced at him with little interest. It had been curried and there was hay in the rick. Was that girl trying to take the place over! He would have to speak to her again. No, he reconsidered ruefully, he had had little luck trying to keep her within limits. It was best to just accept it – for now. She was bound to find other interests to occupy her sooner or later.

Because she certainly wasn't going to. . . .

Besides, she could be a little bit too bossy.

Ben's head came around at the sound of an approaching horse. Squinting into the low sun he saw a tall white horse with a gray mane and tail. He took a minute to recognize the rider. It was Abel McCallister, probably come looking for his daughter. Ben awaited his arrival, hands on his hips.

McCallister swung down from the saddle. Holding the white horse's reins, he extended a gloved hand to Ben. 'Well, I see you're up again. How is it going over here?'

'If you're looking for Kate, she's inside, painting.'

'I know. She told me she was going to do that.

That's not what brings me over, Ben,' McCallister said, tipping his hat back. 'I have an offer to make you.'

'Go ahead,' Ben said warily. The crows had risen in a sudden black cloud at McCallister's approach. Now they settled into the oak again and resumed their scolding. Both men briefly glanced that way.

'I've got two cows that are near to calving. I wondered if you'd be interested in having them,' McCallister said. Ben stared at the rancher uncertainly.

'I don't think I've enough cash on hand to pay you for them,' he answered at length. 'I would be willing to trade a few acres of land for them, if—'

'I've got all the land I need or can use,' McCallister said, brushing away a gnat that had been bothering him. 'I'm willing to trust you for the money. A man has to start somewhere, Ben, and there are few cattle around the Pawnee area. These would at least give you a beginning.'

'Mr McCallister,' Ben said, glancing toward the house and then toward the far skies, 'your daughter and I aren't—'

'This has nothing to do with my daughter,'

McCallister said forcefully. 'I think you're a decent young man trying to make a start on a shoestring. I think you will make it; I think we'll be good neighbors for a lone time.'

All Ben could say was, 'Sure, I'd like to have them. I'll pay you back, McCallister.'

'I know you will.' Briefly he rested a hand on Ben's shoulder. 'You want us to bring them over, or do you want to come and get them?'

'Won't they just wander back to your ranch?'

'Likely,' McCallister said. 'I guess I'll finally have to get around to registering a brand and slapping iron onto my stock. Why don't you consider doing the same thing?'

'It's an idea,' Ben Flowers agreed. 'For now, bring them over if you don't mind. I'm not sure that I can handle the job just yet. And if they wander, well, then they wander.'

'Fine,' McCallister said. 'I'll have Dusty and Hugh push them over sometime today.'

He started to remount and Ben asked, 'Don't you want to talk to Kate before you go?'

'Son,' he replied, 'I've been talking to her for twenty-two years. Not that it ever did much good. . . .' His voice trailed off He glanced at the house, swung into leather and turned his horse southward toward the home ranch.

Ben alternately grinned and frowned as he looked around the property. The clogged well was a reminder of how much work he still had to do. He knew that he was not up to that on this day. But he could look around at the long grass, the gently flowing rill, the lean-to, knowing that the cabin roof was now sound; the cabin's interior was getting into shape. Now he had two cows, and calves on the way, the land and water to provide for them. It had been a struggle – he grimly remembered the Whittaker brothers – but in a relatively short time things had come together. He remembered the dream he had started out with and realized that he was now walking through the middle of it.

'Today?' Elizabeth Cole asked hesitantly, as she watched Rincon belt on his pistol.

'We can't wait any longer, can we? We're broke, the hotel wants its money and so does the stable. It's best to tackle it now. Once I get rid of that nester, we'll have all the time we need to look for that gold. And once we have that, well . . . then we'll shake the dust of this hick town from our boots and get on with living again.'

Elizabeth watched with subdued excitement as Rincon adjusted his gunbelt, placed his black hat on his head and strode toward the door, boot-heels clicking. He had absolute confidence in his ability, and Elizabeth had to have absolute confidence in him. Because if he failed. . . .

She did not even wish to consider that. There was no other option but success. She stood at the window for a while, watching the shabby town come to life. A man would die on this day, but she could dredge up no real sympathy for him.

After all, she barely knew Ben Flowers.

NINE

Rincon had been watching the conversation from behind the screen of sage on the knoll to the west of the ranch. He had no idea what the two men were talking about, and he did not care. What he was waiting for was the big man on the white horse to leave, and after ten minutes or so, he did.

Rincon saw no one else on the property except for the nester, Ben Flowers, but, of course, there might have been. There were two horses in the lean-to stable, but that did not necessarily mean anything. Any number of men had an extra mount. Rincon knew from his days as a Texas cowhand that on trail drives it was a necessity. Two, three or four horses were not uncommon to keep from wearing down your ponies. Still he waited and watched as the greener in the white shirt and blue jeans shuffled around his yard, apparently aimlessly. No one else seemed to be around, still Rincon had not lived as long as he had by being rash. He watched the cabin closely for long minutes more.

Then, drawing his lips tightly together, he decided to brace the nester. Someone else might come by or return from a ranch chore. Besides, Flowers did not know Rincon by sight. Perhaps he could insinuate himself into his confidence, get a feel for matters and then go about his business.

Which was to eliminate Ben Flowers.

Returning to his hidden black horse, Rincon started it at a walk down the grassy knoll.

Ben saw the approaching rider from the corner of his eye and he stood watching as the man approached the cabin. A tall, lean man with dark eyes he was, riding a black horse with three white stockings. The horse moved briskly across the yard. The crows rose again in unison from the oak. Ben thought that he would have to find some way to discourage the birds from nesting there.

Ben Flowers suddenly realized that he was unarmed, but there seemed no need for guns. The man, likely a passing stranger asking for directions, wore a wide smile, and he lifted his hand in greeting as his horse came to a halt, its muscles rippling beneath twitching skin.

'Help you?' Ben asked.

'I don't know,' the stranger answered. 'I hope so. I'm dragging the line, friend. Looking for work.'

'There's none here,' Ben said. 'Nothing I could pay you for anyway.'

'Oh, well,' the stranger shrugged. 'Times are tough all over. I'll keep looking. Could you at least spare me a meal?'

Ben didn't hesitate. In those times on the Great Plains with distances long, with the hard weather, sparse settlements and roving Indians, a hungry man was not turned away. 'I'll see what I can find. Swing on down.'

Rincon did so. He looped the reins to the black loosely around the hitch rail in front of the cabin and followed Ben inside. 'Fixing things up, are you?' Rincon said, glancing around at the fresh paint on the walls.

'Trying to,' Ben replied. 'Let me check the

pantry. . . .' He paused because the all-too distinctive sound of a Colt revolver's hammer being ratcheted back caught his ear, and he spun around to see Rincon's gun trained on him.

'I'm not really hungry, friend,' Rincon said. Any trace of his smile was now gone. 'I just want to know where it is. I assume you've found it by now.'

'Found what?'

'Either you're running a bluff – which isn't very smart – or I'm just going to have to start looking myself. Without you around, Flowers.'

'You know who I am?' Ben asked. From the corner of his eye he saw a shadowy figure easing slowly from the sleeping area, coming ever closer and he silently prayed that she would not make a move. Ben had no doubt that the man he faced was dangerous. more dangerous than the wild-eyed Whittaker brothers by far. There was steely determination in this one's dark eyes. Carefully he said, 'Your name is Rincon, isn't it?'

'Am I that famous,' the gunman laughed, his gun hand still steady, his eyes still menacing.

'I've heard your name in connection with a few things that have been going on.'

'From who? Elizabeth, maybe?'

'Who?' Ben asked blankly, and then it came back to him. 'Elizabeth Cole?'

'That's what she calls herself these days,' Rincon said. 'She doesn't matter now. It's one of two ways, you hand it over or I shoot you. Which way do you want it?'

'Look, Rincon – I'm not even wearing a gun!'

'What's that got to do with anything?' the Texas gunman said.

There was a small noise and a shadowy movement behind him. Rincon's eyes shifted and narrowed. A paint can rolled across the floor of the cabin. Frowning, Rincon returned his gaze to Ben. 'What's that about?' he asked.

'It's about me,' Kate McCallister said. 'Stand where you are. I've got you in the sights of this Winchester.'

Rincon did not move, but he looked toward the bedroom to see a paint-speckled little girl, weighing about ninety pounds, her dark hair cut off unevenly, covering him with a .44-40 rifle. He almost laughed out loud.

'You look like a stiff breeze could blow you away,' he said disparagingly.

'It doesn't take much strength to pull a trigger,' Kate responded. 'I want you out of my house, and I want you out now!'

Rincon wasn't going to give it up. Not now, after five years of waiting, and certainly not under orders from a skinny little prairie girl. He didn't want to kill her, but she had left him little choice. The nester, Ben Flowers, still stood near the fireplace, his hands half-elevated, his eyes filled with anguish. Flowers was not going to give Rincon any trouble. He was unarmed and obviously injured.

Rincon spun toward Kate McCallister and she shot him dead.

Rincon's Colt had fired off first, gouging a furrow in the newly painted walls. But Kate had been steadied, ready for the move, her sights settled on Rincon and the .44-40 slug from the Winchester rifle caught him solidly in the chest. The gunman's knees buckled and he folded up limply. Momentarily he seemed to smile as he clutched at his chest.

'I. . . .' Rincon said. That was the last word he ever spoke.

'Kate!' Ben Flowers said, rushing across the room to take her into his arms. 'He might have killed you.'

'He *would* have killed you. What was I to do, stand by and watch it happen?' Still in his arms she looked up at him with those deep blue eyes. He could feel her shuddering now, as the gravity of what she had done swept over her. He held her until the trembling passed, her head against his chest. The rifle dropped from her limp fingers. 'I don't ever want to have to do anything like that again,' she muttered.

'You won't have to,' Ben answered, lifting her chin with his thumb. 'You won't ever have to fear anything again. I'm going to take care of you from now on, Kate. Don't ask me how, but I will.'

'Will you?' she asked, tilting her head back to look up at him.

'Sure. Don't you remember what you said to Rincon when you braced him? "I want you out of *my* house." Well, it is yours too now, Kate. It's our house from here on.'

Elizabeth Cole had her suitcase packed. No matter what happened, she knew that today was the day she would have to flee Pawnee. She could see out the window as she sat on the bed, watching and waiting for Rincon's return. The sun was high when he made it back to the little town.

A buckboard driven by a slender, dark-haired girl trailed in. Beside her sat Ben Flowers. Behind the wagon a black horse with three white stockings was tethered, and in the bed of the wagon there was a shapeless something covered with canvas. She rose and searched the room for anything she might have left behind, wondering if there was a way to sneak out of the hotel past the manager. She still had her paint pony and much of her youth.

There was always another man, another town.

Spring passed slowly into summer. Both of the cows had delivered their calves. Each had been carrying twins. Ben Flowers watched them wade through the long grass to reach the silver rill, smiling as the calves would kick up their heels as if delighted to he alive. So this was what it was like to start a herd, a home.

Contrary to what they had expected, the cows had never shown an inclination to stray back to McCallister's range. Cows needed little to be satisfied, and they had it where they were now. Ben and Abel McCallister had again conferred and discussed the advisability of registering brands. There would come a time in the future when it would only be prudent if Ben's herd increased as he hoped.

'You can use my bull when you judge they're ready again,' McCallister offered.

'I appreciate that. I'll let you know.'

McCallister was at Ben's ranch the day the wagon from Pawnee arrived and two husky townsmen flipped back the tarp covering their load and moved the double bed into the house. Of pecan wood with a highly polished headboard it took up almost all of the sleeping area. Abel McCallister smiled wryly, shook his head and headed his horse homeward again.

The wedding was a month later.

McCallister attended, wearing a suit and tight collar. Hugh and Dusty were there and a newly arrived settler named Heath, his wife and daughter along with a few of the townspeople they had gotten to know.

Ben barely got through the ceremony. His legs trembled half the time. Kate, on the other hand, took everything as a matter of course, and still wearing her white wedding dress with the blue ribbons, she bustled about serving her guests, chatting away merrily.

Ben had to go out onto the porch and sit, breathing heavily, watching the distances. He felt more than heard Abel Whittaker sag onto the porch beside him. The cattleman's hand rested on Ben's shoulder.

'You didn't make a mistake, son. These things just take a little getting used to. She'll be a good wife.'

'I know that. It just now seems . . . so sudden,' Ben said without looking at his father-in-law.

'Sudden?' McCallister said with a smile. 'Son, the rest of us knew it was going to happen from the first day you got here.'

'I guess I still don't know much about women,' Ben said, glancing at Abel McCallister.

'You'll learn, son. You're about to learn a lot – and you've got a good teacher in there. Why don't you go back in and stand by her?'

Ben nodded and rose, still a little wobbly on his feet. 'One other thing I noticed,' Abel said with a restrained smile, 'don't you think she's starting to fill out some now?'

Whatever misgivings Ben had were dispelled in the following weeks. Everything was twice as easy, everything gave him more pleasure. He was more pleased with his work. In the morning coffee would be on before he had stretched and risen from his new bed. Supper was cooked for him – and not his sort of cooking which involved grabbing what he could and jamming it down. In the evenings they usually sat on the porch and watched the sundown skies, just holding hands, saying little. They didn't need to say much.

On Sundays now Abel McCallister usually came over for chicken dinner. He seemed every bit as pleased with the state of affairs as the young people did. After dinner he and Ben would sit at the table, discussing the crops, the chances of rain, the cattle. He always left early so as not to intrude on their private time.

Things, Ben reflected when he had the time, had not only turned out as he had hoped, but much better. He had everything a man could want, although he had hopes of building the ranch up further and turning it into a really prosperous spread.

That was on the first day of June.

On the second day of June, Calvin Mercer returned.

TEN

His leg had been a long time recovering. Always a bitter man, Calvin Mercer was now even more so. He sat his bulky roan horse, rubbing the stump of his missing right arm, and adjusted himself in the saddle to take the load off his gunshot leg which still troubled him. The injury had left him with a heavy limp.

Someone would have to pay for that.

They had tossed him out of the hotel and for a time he had slept in the boarding-house before they evicted him from there as well. Lately he had been sleeping on the plains with one thin blanket and his saddle for a pillow.

Rincon had somehow gotten himself shot dead. Considering how good the Texan was with his guns, that was quite a surprise. Elizabeth had slipped away, which was all right with Cal Mercer. He had never liked the haughty little blonde anyway. She had sold Rincon's black horse for getaway money and gone off to wherever women like her went when they were turning the page. He spent little time thinking about Elizabeth Cole.

He spent a lot of time, on the other hand, thinking about what was owed him: twenty thousand in gold. Small recompense for the loss of an arm and five years of his life, but if he could recover the money he would call it even.

Now he sat watching the ranch below, amazed at the transformation. A window had been cut into the face of the front wall. There were white-painted chairs on the porch, flowers planted inside a circle of rocks. The lean-to had been patched together and a small herd of cattle grazed peacefully on the long grass; a flock of brown hens pecked around the front yard. He wasn't really surprised.

A man could do a lot with twenty-thousand, and the nester was obviously doing just that.

Except it was Cal Mercer's money!

He was the one who had set up Billy Carter to open the safe. He was the one who had spent bitter cold nights and days out on the long plains running from the army. There was a time when a man just had to stand up and take back what was rightfully his. Still he thought matters over cautiously – cautiously for Sudden Calvin Mercer.

He did not intend to make the same mistake Rincon had.

'Well, the creek's running dry,' Ben said at the breakfast table. 'I guess I can't put it off any longer. We have to have that well cleaned out.'

'It's a dirty job,' Kate said as she refilled his coffee cup. 'And grueling.'

'That's why I kept putting it off, but there's no choice, not if we intend to have clean water over the summer dry spell.'

'*I* intend to,' Kate said firmly and Ben laughed.

'Then guess who's going to have to help me?'

'I can't imagine,' she said with mock puzzlement. Then, 'I'll get this dress off and change into my ranch-hand's gear and we can get started when you're ready.'

Ben watched appreciatively as she went into the

sleeping area, now with a hung door, slipped out of her dress and house shoes and started to rig up for the day's labor. It was such a small pleasure watching her dress, but a very real one.

And, he considered, Abel Whittaker had been right she was beginning to fill out.

'We have a plan, right?' Kate asked, standing hands on her hips, staring at the covered well.

'We do. I'm going down with a shovel, you're cranking up the muck.' As he spoke he was winding the new hemp rope around the spool of the windlass. The old, rotten rope he threw aside. He fixed the new galvanized bucket he had purchased in Pawnee to the rope with bolted steel clamps, tested it and pronounced himself satisfied.

'This isn't going to be an easy day, Kate,' he told her, as he placed his hat aside and stripped off his shirt.

'I already kinda knew that,' Kate said dryly. 'Let's do what we can, right? If one or both of us gets too tired, we can come back in the morning. There's no real rush now, is there?'

'Not now.' He walked behind the house and returned with the pole ladder he had been using to patch the roof. The ancient contraption still seemed sound.

'Is that long enough to reach the bottom of the well?' Kate asked, looking uneasy for the first time.

'I guess we'll find out.' Upending the ladder they tilted it into the well. The stench of muck rose heavily into the clear skies. 'I guess a lot can collect in five years,' Ben said. Looking down he could watch the semi-solid ground suck the feet of the ladder into the mire.

'What if the ladder keeps sinking?' Kate asked.

'Then,' Ben said with an uneasy grin, 'I'll have to count on you to crank me up out of the well.'

He swung one leg over, tested his weight on the ladder, took his shovel in one hand and grabbed on to the ladder with the other. Cautiously he eased his way down into the dark depths of the well. Looking up he could see Kate's anxious face watching his descent.

The air was fetid; slime and moss covered the stone sides of the well. He wondered if he would have been better off simply beginning a new one. It was a little too late for such thoughts now. Shirtless, the unstable ladder his only firm handhold, he went farther into the rank depths of the well.

Reaching the last available rung he poked around with the shovel, searching for a place that offered some sort of support to keep him from slipping away into the mud. Mercifully he found something. The blade of the shovel rang off stone, and Ben guessed that the original digger of the well – whoever that might have been – had been wise enough to construct a rocky ledge at ladder depth. Perhaps the problem of accumulating debris in the well had a long history.

He nevertheless eased off the ladder cautiously, his back pressed to the wall of the well. 'All right, Kate!' he called up in a voice that echoed up to her. 'Lower the bucket' This was going to be a rotten day.

He heard the windlass creaking on its newly oiled axle and saw the bucket making its way downward. When it had reached him, Ben placed it aside and, wiping the back of his hand across his eyes where perspiration had gathered, started to work.

He had taken two strokes with his shovel, scooping the muck into the new bucket, when the blade of the implement struck metal. Frowning, he bent forward as far as he dared and cleared some mud away from his discovery.

It was, of course, the old bucket which had been deserted by rotten ropes and time. Prying it up out of the mud proved a more difficult task than he had expected. Sure, it would be full of mud, but even when he was reduced to placing the shovel handle over his knee to use it as fulcrum base, the old object was incredibly heavy.

Finally the bucket was released from the sucking muck and Ben grabbed the handle and tried to move it aside. It was still heavy. Very heavy. He bent to examine the bucket, sucked in his breath, dumped the slime out of the new bucket Kate had lowered and fitted the old one inside.

'Haul away, Kate! I'm coming up.'

'Already?' she asked with concerned surprise. Leaving his shovel behind, Ben gripped the rough rungs of the old pole ladder and began ascending toward daylight as Kate continued to work the windlass's crank. He appeared not many moments after she had gotten the pail to the rim of the well and swung it aside.

'What is it?' Kate asked, as the mud-spattered Ben Flowers swung a leg up and over the low rim and walked to her.

He crouched, dug around inside the slime-soaked bucket for a minute and then stood, holding a rotten section of leather. A buckle could be seen on one side. The object was heavier than it had a right to he.

'The cause of all of our troubles, I think,' Ben said. Wiping away some of the mud he nodded as if to himself and said to Kate, 'Rotted old saddle-bags.' He managed to pry one of the buckles open and dip his hand into the pocket of the bags. His hand lifted again and there was something small and round between his fingers. He grabbed his shirt to wipe it, and with each brush of the cloth the article grew brighter until it rested in Ben's palm as clean and bright as the day it was minted.

'Gold,' Kate said breathlessly.

'It is, indeed, and there's more of it.'

By now Ben had heard enough of the rumors, learned enough from his own encounters to hazard a guess at what had happened:

'We know that the army lost a great deal of gold from its safe at Fort Mandan. How it was taken, we will never discover. But we know that among the gang that took it was Rincon – the man you shot. Why did strangers keep returning here? What were the men looking for who tore up the floorboards in the house – the gold, of course.'

'That would have been a better hiding place,' Kate said, leaning back against the stone wall around the well. Ben rested beside her, the gold coin still bright in his hand catching sunlight and seeming to trap it.

'It would have been if the thieves lived here, but they didn't. The Whittaker brothers owned this place and, as we know, all of them were dangerous. Someone among the thieves needed to hide the gold quickly before the Whittakers saw it, yet somewhere it could be quickly recovered if they had to make a run for it.'

'Down the well, in the bucket,' Kate said.

Ben nodded, 'Yes. Then if the robbers decided they had to make a run for it, it would only take a matter of minutes for them to run to the well, crank up the bucket and retrieve the gold.'

'But things did not work out for them.'

'No, they didn't. The army tracked them

down and all hell broke loose – witness the front of our cabin. The army must have searched but could not find it. Rincon and the others – whoever they were – were either killed or taken off to prison. The two Whittaker brothers living here were also dead. I doubt they ever knew about the gold. No matter – the place fell into disrepair over a five-year period. Timbers sagged, ropes rotted away.

'Some around here believe that the men who were with that army unit came back, tearing up the place to search for the gold. Rincon was certainly searching for it. The Whittakers – well, I believe they just wanted their hideout back. And revenge on whoever had shot their brothers.'

'How many men have died for this, Ben?' Kate asked, as he handed her the shiny fifty-dollar goldpiece. He didn't answer.

He saw the bulky figure of the one-armed man as he eased around the lean-to toward them, a pistol in his meaty hand.

'You figured it all out pretty good, nester,' Calvin Mercer said. 'I've been listening. You didn't get it all right, but that's about what happened. Now, if you don't mind, I'd like my gold back.'

Kate stepped forward, her small hands clenched. 'Who are you and what makes this yours? This is our property. What are you doing here?'

Calvin Mercer glanced at the skinny kid in the red shirt and dismissed him as a threat. He stepped toward the rotting saddle-bags, keeping his gun trained on Ben Flowers.

'You can't do that!' the kid shouted lunging forward. Mercer slashed at the kid with the barrel of his Colt. Kate fell to the ground, stunned. A streak of crimson lined her forehead.

Enraged, Ben leaned forward. Mercer, bending to collect the saddle-bags, half-rose and turned back to face Ben, but it was too late. Ben was on him, swinging and yelling wild curses. The one-armed man tried to fight back, but Ben was inside, under his arm, and he could not strike down with his pistol. He triggered off one shot, and it flew into the lean-to, startling the two horses there.

Ben's ears rang with the close thunder of the gun, but he did not slow down his assault. He winged a right-hand blow that bounced off Mercer's temple, dug two lefts into his ribcage.

Mercer backed away, unable to do much to stop the assault. As long as Ben kept on top of him, beneath Cal's arm, no shot was really possible.

Furiously, Mercer continued to strike down with his pistol barrel, but Ben's head, against the big man's chest, was an elusive target. Mercer felt his legs thud against the low stone wall of the well, felt himself go off-balance, and he fought back almost maniacally, dropping his pistol in his attempt to save himself.

Ben's assault was relentless. This man, this *thing* had clubbed down Kate, and he fought on with blind fury throwing wild lefts and rights to Calvin Mercer's head and body. He realized that Mercer was tilting away from him and that the big man's hand was grasping at Ben for balance.

Ben pulled back quickly to avoid the groping hand and watched as Calvin Mercer tipped over and fell headfirst into the well. He landed with a sickening thud in the mud and mire far below. Ben took a deep breath and looked down. Mercer was unmoving, his head twisted in a strange angle, his one visible eye staring blankly at the shaft.

Kate was suddenly beside him, unsteady on her feet, her forehead streaked with blood. She put her arm around Ben and peered into the well.

'I think he broke his neck,' Ben said.

In a tone of voice Ben had never heard Kate use before or after, she spat, 'Good!' and turned away toward the cabin.

ELEVEN

The army finally did come through with a reward for the recovery of the stolen gold – fifteen per cent. Not a lot, maybe, but it allowed Ben and Kate to pay Abel McCallister back for his help. There was enough left to purchase a mule to plow with, and they started putting the seed corn into the ground. A little late in the year, but with luck the crop would be fine. For no reason at all, except that they had gotten tired of strangers arriving unannounced, Kate came home one day with a yellow mongrel pup – shaggy and ugly. Whatever it had been bred out of, its huge paws showed that it would grow into a large watch dog. It padded after Kate wherever she went, tongue lolling with contentment.

Ben sat on the porch at sunset, watching the constantly shifting colors – orange, vermilion and deep purple. Looking at the land – his land – he reflected. His dream had not come easily. Nothing had gone the way his imagination had projected it would happen. But it had come. He was a lucky man. He had paid a price, but had been richly rewarded for any sacrifice.

Richly.

Kate came out of the house to sit beside him. The big pup settled contentedly at her feet. The skies continued to darken. Soon they would re-enter their warm cabin, and later when it was time to turn the lanterns down they would fall into their big new, comfortable bed. Kate took his hand.

'What are you thinking about?' she asked quietly.

'Nothing much,' Ben told his wife.

'Just daydreaming?'

'That's it,' Ben said, smiling at her, 'just dreaming.'